HOMECOMING

"Don't fight it, Granthan," Colonel Kayle's image croaked. "You penetrated planetary defenses, God knows how, but we have you pinpointed."

I felt cold sweat on my forehead. "You've got to listen, Kayle!" I shouted. "Recall your missiles! *I've got the key that can win the war—*"

"Sorry, Granthan," Kayle said. "It's too late—even if I could take the chance that you were still on our side."

"Stow that, you pompous idiot!" I barked. "I'm no spy!"

I flipped the switch, sat gripping the couch, my stomach rising with each heave of the floating capsule. Despite the medikit, pain screamed through my broken leg, fractured skull, and charred arm. I was ten miles offshore from Key West. The missiles would hit in five minutes.

And if I died, so would mankind.

END
AS A
HERO

KEITH
LAUMER

ACE SCIENCE FICTION BOOKS
NEW YORK

END AS A HERO

An Ace Science Fiction Book/published by arrangement with
the author

PRINTING HISTORY
Ace edition/August 1985

For information address: The Berkley Publishing Group,
200 Madison Avenue, New York, New York 10016.

ISBN: 0-441-20656-5

Ace Science Fiction Books are published by
The Berkley Publishing Group,
200 Madison Avenue, New York, New York 10016.
PRINTED IN THE UNITED STATES OF AMERICA

. . . the worst thing in life . . . to try to please, and please not.

—Arab proverb

The best thing in the world is to do good by stealth and be found out by accident.

—Harold Lamb

CHAPTER ONE

1

On a world of the star known to medieval astronomer/
astrologers as "The Armpit of the Central One," an
event occurred. It was an event of which only one
being was aware: one torpid intelligence which had
spent most of its long existence in a state of total
sensory deprivation. But into the long silence and
darkness of its semiconsciousness there now came a
shocking intrusion, shattering a vivid dream of times
long gone.

The touch was so faint as to seem but a vagary of
imagination, a tactile sensation of infinite subtlety, as
insubstantial as the idle thoughts which were the entity's
sole remaining activity. And yet, the Gool reasoned
solemnly, *something* had occurred; had it not, one
would not now be awake off-schedule, pondering the
nature of the event which had intruded on the dream

of vanished glories. In its deep pit the gelatinous bulk of the entity stirred, a ripple passing spontaneously through it, settling it even more securely against the confines of its immemorial nest. Involuntarily, it communicated its unrest to the Others of its Kind, each in its pit, linked by a cable of living tissue to the Great One, occupying the Brain Pit, and by a tube—all that remained of the ancestral vertebrate body-plan—to the Eating Trough, where the appendages of the Others jostled for space, each blind "head" sucking in the watery globigerinous ooze that had long ago drained from the bed of the dying sea into the low area of a former Deep.

Even as it fed hungrily, the Gool examined the ghostly touch it had felt for an instant, eidetically reviewing the curious pattern:

"—not sure, but I think it was a contact..."

Its faint residual capacity for curiosity now aroused to sluggish action, the Gool concentrated its awareness on an analysis of this strange new thing. Then it focused its full attention, tracing down every outré characteristic of the alien thought-form.

Abruptly, the Gool experienced the long-forgotten sensation of astonishment: This thing could not be: here was no random vagary of one's own nerve-mass. Fully intrigued now, it followed up the lead—and quailed at the shock of the brilliant burst of pseudo-light into which it had smashed unsuspecting.

LINK UP, MY MASTERS, the Gool yelled silently to its fellows. Not for many millennia had the entity felt the impulse to communicate. The others, though bewildered, responded at once, reaching out blindly, filtering immensity for some hint of Contact.

2

In the disciplinary tank aboard the Terrestrial Space Arm Ship *Tiglath-Pileser,* 500 guns, Fleet Admiral Hayle commanding, Spaceman Last Class Freddy Tsaio-Ping awoke from a deep sleep with a yell that brought the deck cop snoozing in a broken chair fifty feet along the way to his feet, shock gun in hand.

"Awright, who's the wise guy?" he demanded defensively; if old Carbuncle had caught him napping— or even that green half-striper—good-bye retirement. He squinted into the darkness, heard a sound and went toward it.

Freddy Tsaio-Ping was on his feet, clutching the barred door, his head against the bars, sobbing as if heartbroken.

". . . enough," he said brokenly. "You promised. If I was good all day, you wouldn't . . ."

"If I didn't know you got no booze in there, Freddy," the noncom said almost gently, "I'd say you was on a crying jag. Buck up, boy, whassamare?"

Freddy turned away his tear-streaked face. "Dunno," he muttered. "Bad dream, I guess." He shivered, though it was not cold in the D-tank. "I'm okay now," he said more firmly, then abruptly sobbed. "Need me some light in here, Sarge," he said. "In the dark it's no good."

"See what I can do, Fred. Now you just take it easy; no more yelling and carrying on." The NCO walked away, and in the dark cell Freddy Tsaio-Ping fought down the recurrent sobs.

3

WHAT IMPUDENCE IS THIS—A TRICK TO USURP MY PLACE? LINK WELL, MY MASTERS! the Great One boomed silently to its bewildered subordinates, its handful of fellow survivors of the days of Gool greatness.

Thoroughly intrigued now, feeding forgotten, the entities examined the new thing that had come so unexpectedly to shatter the immemorial routine of their static lives. Long had it been since the concept of a non-Gool life-form had been forgotten. Their universe thus transformed, they at once launched all their combined probe capacity along the fragile pathway of Contact, to explore and examine wonder on wonder. Tentatively, they poked and meddled at random, observing the results. Slowly the nature of what they had stumbled upon became more clear to the naive Gool, and with the swiftness of ancient instinct triggered, they/it evoked a plan—and at once implemented it, and dismissed the matter to return to the chore of feeding.

4

On the Staff Duty desk aboard TSA *Belshazzar,* the new *Colossus*-class Survey vessel on a routine trans-Plutonian sweep of Home Sector, Duty NCOIC Spaceman First Class Lou Hybrams stretched and yawned noisily, both bored with the uneventful night-duty hours, and alert for the peremptory blast of the Incoming-Classified squawker. Be just his luck to catch a new exercise while the SDO was off to chow.... Suddenly his slack expression changed to one of astonishment. He made an abortive move toward the Panic button, but checked and looked down, frowning at his trembling right hand.

"You goin' in business fer yerself, or what?" he muttered half aloud. Then, as if suddenly remembering a duty undone, he rose briskly from the chair on which he had been perched and went across to the Security Blue panel and with an almost defiant air, grasped the seal and broke it away. Lifting the panel door, he looked in wonderment at the array of emergency switches—by sacred TSA Regulation Number One, never seen since they were installed in the command subassembly at Scapa Flow, by any other than the admiral commanding. Cautiously, wanting to fight the impulse, but somehow carried away by a mood of defiance, he reached out and slammed down the big knife in the center of the array, and in the instantaneous darkness and silence, heard himself scream for just a moment before the deck smashed him into unconsciousness.

5

In his second-floor office at the Psychodynamics Institute, Peter Granthan shook his head.

"Sorry, Reed. Even if your theory is correct—which I doubt, as I've told you in perfect candor—I still don't think I'm the man for the job."

"Peter, you're the best we've got," the elderly chief of section countered. "You're the only man under thirty who ever took an honors degree in psychodynamics—to say nothing of your brilliant dissertation on precisely the techniques involved here. You, Peter, are already, at your age, regarded with a sort of awe by your colleagues. The concept of the Personality Fraction in itself—"

"You do me too much honor, Reed," Granthan said easily. "If my contributions are to be of any value, others must be able to use them as effectively as I. No doubt there are plenty of bright young fellows who'd leap at the chance to save the world in full view of the cameras."

"Peter—I've counted on you. From the beginning I've assumed—"

"Too much, Reed," Granthan said gently. "I'm not actually thoroughly convinced that the alleged peril exists. After all, what have we got? A number of rather hysterical reports from fleet units in Deep Space of a crew member running amok, wrecking his ship, or trying to, and afterwards babbling hysterically of the ghoul, G-O-O-L, as the media prefer to spell it."

"There's a good deal more to it than that, Peter, as you well know," Reed said sternly. "We have a highly objective report by David Blake of Princeton, who shipped out as ship's psychologist aboard *Belshazzar* last year. He's a sound man. He reported an abortive contact attempt which he personally experienced. I'm sure you recall it: fascinating reading."

"But still only reading," Granthan said in a patient tone. "Got Dave plenty of publicity, too, as I recall: 'Prominent Shrink Repels Mind Attack.' Helped circulation, no doubt."

"Have you talked to David, Peter?" Reed inquired intently.

Granthan nodded. "Poor fellow was quite upset: 'A ton of liver at the bottom of a dark well,' was one of his more lucid phrases. Good thing the media didn't get hold of that one. But what they did get was plenty: 'Mental Invasion by Space Monsters.' And now you propose that this Institute join in the circus. You surprise me, Dr. Bates." Granthan frowned. "Psychodynamics itself is not yet so firmly established as a legitimate discipline as to be invulnerable to ridicule. A fiasco at this point could wipe out most of what's been accomplished here in the past twenty years."

"There will be no fiasco, Peter," Reed said solemnly. "I'm quite ready to stake my reputation and my professional career on that."

"Your career and my neck," Granthan murmured, then immediately apologized: "Theory is a fine thing, Reed, but we need another twenty years of intensive research before we'll be ready to march out with banners blaring and trumpets flying, to rescue the planet." He leaned back, as one who has concluded a conversation. "'And there's an end on't' as Dr. Johnson would say, and often did," he added.

"Peter, forget the banners and bugles. General Titus is as anxious as you to avoid publicity."

"I don't understand how you ever got that old devil to sit still long enough to refuse to listen," Granthan said. "You're a persuasive fellow, Reed: 'General, I just want to send one of my boys along to watch how you carry out your orders to get to the bottom of this Mind Invasion business, and if you flunk out, he'll step in and use his butterfly net to round up the enemy. Okay?' Something like that, Reed?"

"I wasn't quite so facetious as that," Reed Bates replied with a faint smile. "I pointed out that in the event that it appeared there was some factual basis for all the hysteria, it wouldn't hurt to have on board a specialist in such matters—matters that a practical spaceman could not be expected to have studied at the Academy."

"I'll bet he loved that, Reed," Granthan said, smiling.

"In any event, he agreed," the older man said with finality. "Subject to your full security clearance, of course." Reed got to his feet, nodded curtly.

"Since you decline, Peter, I shall undertake to make other arrangements, though I confess I'm disappointed. Bitterly disappointed." His voice quavered momentarily on the last words.

"I've got the feeling," Granthan said almost accusingly, "that if I don't take on this harebrained stunt, *you* will." He rose. "All right, you old blackmailer, I volunteer. Which way do I go?"

6

"I make no secret of it," the stocky, blunt-featured man with the eagle on his starched collar said grumpily. "I consider this entire affair to be sensational nonsense dreamed up and kept alive by unprincipled journalists. However, I have not been called upon to make a decision regarding the advisability of involving the fleet in a publicity campaign. You have survived a National Agency Check: my job is to determine the security risk represented by a stranger who is proposed as supercargo aboard a ship of the line. I have done so." After an ominous pause, the colonel thrust out his hand. "Congratulations, Professor Granthan—you managed to keep your signature off every one of the five hundred and seventy-three treasonous declarations on my list."

Granthan pressed the hard-callused hand briskly and dropped it. "It's nice to know someone is keeping track of the sophomoric activities of my youth, Colonel Kayle. Or is it?"

7

In the Brain Pit, the Great One, who combined in its person all that remained of the rank and power that had once ruled an empire among the stars, noticing the continued activity of his slaves, stirred himself, feeling, though dimly, the need for some affirmative action. Summoning all of its once-mighty powers, it scanned the shrunken exocosm, perceiving the new pattern impinging on the old, the traditional one so long-established, noting points of Contact *here* and *here*, and grasping at once the shape of the needed counteraction. Swiftly, it commanded the total attention of its pitifully few remaining subjects, the sadly degenerate relicts of lesser lords, ordering them to discontinue their fumbling efforts at once, lest they alarm without neutralizing this disturbing new force invading Gool reality. NOW, he imposed the absolute upon them, they must make use of their aeons-old wisdom, born of long experience as commanders of worlds and of irresistible battle fleets in the Great Years of their almost-forgotten youth.

NO MORE AIMLESS BLUNDERING, BUT WITH PRECISION, the Great One ordered. A PRESSURE HERE, A BLOW STRUCK YONDER, THE MEREST TOUCH *THERE*: it communicated to their minds a pattern at a level infinitely more subtle than the verbal. Their responses, though sluggish by comparison with their full powers, came within a fraction of a microsecond:

AND *THIS* NEXUS, ONLY DEVELOPING.

HERE IS THE DANGER. AND HERE.

A SUBTLE STROKE AT *THIS* INTERSECTION OF VEC-TORS. AND *HERE* I PERCEIVE A PLANE OF WEAK-NESS. . . .

The Great One integrated their contributions and at once computed the resultant course of action. To each underling it assigned a task, and without pause they turned to their duties.

8

In a bright-lit office high in an old building of ugly red stone, Peter Granthan shook his head, frowning. His expression was like that of a man coming suddenly on a vista of unexplored valleys and of distant peaks.

"I'm not sure," he said, half to himself. "But *something* happened. Something new, not like those gassy structures last year. This time it's no accidental configuration—if I got what I think I got."

Dr. Reed Bates, seated across the desk from Granthan, nodded eagerly. "Anything we could record, perhaps with the new compound array?" he inquired in a hopeful tone. Granthan started, as if surprised to discover that he was not alone. He shook his head.

"I'm afraid not, Reed," he said in a tired voice. "There's nothing . . . substantive; just whatever it was that happened under my haircut. Nothing to show the press—or even hint about at the next booze-and-campus-politics brawl."

"You're tired, Peter; and that is hardly the proper terminology to employ with reference to the cocktail reception to which the director has been so gracious as to invite the staff this evening."

Granthan groaned. *"This* evening, Reed? My God, I need two weeks' sleep before I'll have the energy to go to bed." He shuddered rather violently. "No more bad dreams," he stated firmly. "I've been getting into Fifth Level," he explained to his colleague. "Tonight I'm going to split off another personality fraction to keep me out of there. Reed, did you ever fall down a chimney upside down, and get jammed there with your head between your knees?" He tried a casual chuckle which emerged as an uncertain groan.

"Peter, you mustn't become too closely involved personally with this problem," Bates said sternly. "Instead of these lonely vigils, why not think about my proposal—if General Titus hasn't managed to pull enough strings to get it canceled. He doesn't have much time left to work. *Belshazzar* announced for departure on Sunday next."

"That's a notable non sequitur, Doctor," Granthan commented. "Do we have any basis for the assumption that a man in Deep Space is more vulnerable—or more likely to be attacked—than anyone else?"

Bates looked grave. "General Titus unbent so far as to show me a document prepared by his personal staff, suggestions that the recorded 'contacts' so far fall into a pattern which is not in conflict with the ATTAC II theoretical 'worst case' forecast."

For the first time Granthan showed interest. "Ye gods," he said. "No wonder Old Tight-ass decided to go along. That's the program that assumes a 'total war' initiation by an intelligence of magnitude eight, right?"

Bates nodded bleakly. "Of course, the existence of such a fantastically potent compound mind is itself a highly theoretic concept—but the congruency of the staff analysis with the phase one forecast is far from encouraging. Peter, we're in trouble. If this is what it appears to be, the human race is about to lose its patent on the universe."

Granthan nodded. "Come to think of it, I've always wanted to find out firsthand if all the stories about how bad life is aboard a ship of the line are true."

Bates smiled and extended his hand. "Fine business, Peter. I'll notify the colonel at once."

9

"Damned nonsense," the lean, white-mustached man with the six stars on his stiffly starched shirt collar said. He cleared his throat, spat in a metal wastebasket beside his desk and repeated the remark:

"Damned nonsense."

The three newsmen clustered rather nervously before him put their heads together briefly, while standing with pencils ostentatiously poised.

"May I quote that, General?" the red-haired one asked in a nervous voice.

"Boy, do you imagine that I made myself available to you fellows so that I could sit here and say things I wanted kept secret?" the general barked. "And don't be so damned careful when you speak to me. Do like I do: speak your mind. You're not in uniform, so I can't have you shot, you know." General Titus abruptly shoved back his chair and rose, turned and went to the window, tilted the light-control lever and glared out at the immense TSA base spread below.

"He's the only man in the world who can 'stride' three feet," the plump reporter whispered to his colleagues.

"And the old son of a bitch has hearing like a bat," the general said, without turning. "Look down there: all that, a ten-billion-dollar complex dithering like an old maid's tea party because Harlowe Goober wants to sell a few million newspapers. Damned outrage." He turned and resumed his chair.

"Take a look, I said," he growled. The three men went to the window like chastened schoolboys and dutifully looked down at the drab streets and colorless prefab buildings.

"General Titus," the long-haired reporter spoke up clearly. "Since you consider the Gool threat to be nonsense, why have you approved sending some kind of psychologist along with Admiral Hayle?"

"Do your homework, boy," Titus snapped. "This Granthan is a psychodynamicist, best in the business."

"Isn't it true, sir," the redhead joined in, "that you once referred to psychodynamics as 'damned mumbo jumbo'?" The fellow's bright look faded to a slack expression of alert stupidity under the frosty glare with which the baited officer fixed him.

"Maybe so, Junior. So what?" the general snarled.

"Well, General Titus," the bald reporter stepped in. "Some people might consider that to be an inconsistency."

"As I said, buster, 'So what?'" The general shifted his gaze to the redhead, who said nothing.

"Not going to speak up on behalf of consistency?" Titus demanded.

"Sure, General, sir, if that's what the general wants." The man paused to swallow.

"Look," Titus said in a reasonable tone, "if you fellows came up here this afternoon just to see if you could get a rise out of me, consider your mission accomplished." He turned his attention to the desk, where he resumed his seat and picked up a paper from among those spread on the green GI blotter.

"Look at this, now," he muttered. "My security people are getting on the bandwagon. I'd call that a little premature, on Colonel Kayle's part—for a fellow who's looking for a star." Titus glanced at the redhead. "I'm talking to myself, now," he said. "Off the record. I wouldn't want any eavesdropping." He got to his feet.

"Give me an enemy I can shoot at," he said. "All this crap about alien mind attacks is ridiculous—or it would be if I didn't keep getting reports from some of my best field officers backing up the tabloids. Well, if this is the way it is—if this is what I have to fight— okay. These spooks—or ghouls—or whatever—will soon find out that Admiral-General Lloyd B. Titus is the wrong fellow to mess around with. You can quote me on that."

"Sir," the redheaded journalist said earnestly, "may I say that shipping this Granthan out with Hayle—"

"That's Admiral Hayle, sonny," Titus cut in.

"Yessir . . . with Admiral Hayle is the beginning of a counteroffensive against the Gool, meeting them on their own terms?"

"I can't stop you," Titus grated.

"Oh, boy," the bushy-haired one said.

10

Granthan was still tossing things into his new Samsonite Crown Prince Universal ("a damned big suitcase," as the ads said), when his apartment door buzzer sounded. A glance at the screen showed him a pink-cheeked boy in an old-fashioned navy-blue turtleneck. Wearily, Granthan let him in, was instantly informed that his caller was Subensign Wallace Rockford (of the Portland Rockfords) and was here to assist Dr. Granthan with whatever chores needed doing. Granthan told him to sit down and take a few deep breaths.

"Portland, Maine?" Granthan inquired casually after the young officer had smoothed his trouser creases and hairdo. The lad nodded brightly. "Senator Rockford is my uncle," he added. "Dad is mayor now, you know."

"Sorry," Granthan said. "I don't follow ceremonial politics."

"Then maybe *this* will mean something to you," the lad said behind Granthan, who had returned to his packing. At the other's tone, he turned, to see a Navy-issue power gun gripped in the young fellow's hand, and pointed directly at Granthan's face from a range of three feet.

"Oh, sure, now there's a *good* idea," Granthan commented with a casual smile as he took a step toward Subensign Rockford, who said breathlessly, "Close enough."

Granthan nodded. "Too close, in fact, for any really useful work with that tool." As he spoke, he brought his left arm around in an easy but very quick arc and caught they boy's gun hand just above the wrist. A swift pivot and he had jerked the boy to him, dropped his right arm over the other's and levered it with his forearm. The gun fell to the carpet. Granthan kicked it away, as the young officer's face writhed and he burst into tears.

"I . . . it was . . . I can't . . ." he babbled. Granthan nodded and spoke soothingly, released his arm and led him to a deep chair.

"Just take a few deep breaths, Wally," he said in the authoritative tones of a therapist dealing with a routine case. He went to the small bar to the left of the entry hall, quickly mixed a tall glass of something pale green, with ice, and handed it to the subensign. Casually, he picked up the gun, ejected the core, and tossed it into a handy wastebasket. Rockford, still sobbing, his face tear-streaked, accepted the drink and took a large gulp, then looked up at Granthan and spoke more firmly.

"I don't know what got into me, sir," he said. "Just all of a sudden it seemed like such a good idea."

"You always bring along a Mark III when you come calling?" Granthan inquired without emphasis. Rockford looked puzzled for a moment.

"Those were my orders, sir," he explained. "I was to steal—take it from the O.D. room and keep it out of sight, until . . ." He broke off, looking confused.

"Orders to shoot me, Wally, or just scare me to death?"

"Oh, to shoot, sir," Wally said earnestly, nodding. "It was just . . ." His voice trailed off, and his expression was one of vacant horror. Granthan spoke quietly to the lad, and assured him that it was over now, that he could relax, relax. . . .

". . . night," Rockford said. "Orders were very specific about that. No questions, he said. Just be sure to take the gun, and as soon as you turned your back— it was awful, sir," the subensign blurted, near tears again. Granthan quieted him, little by little extracted the account of the midnight visitation by the faceless man who had entered the VOQ room to awaken the young officer and assign to him his solemn mission.

"—so am I going crazy?" Rockford wailed. "Nobody can get past that desk officer without competent orders. And even so, nobody could get into my quarters without breaking two class-one time locks. So"— he gulped and looked up earnestly at Granthan—"none of it makes sense."

"You've been hearing about the so-called Gool attacks on our fleet units, Wally," Granthan said. "This is what they were talking about."

Rockford looked stricken. "But—sir, the media aren't going to hear about this, uh, incident, are they?"

Granthan looked keenly at the earnest young fellow. "Since your fainting spell half an hour ago," he said, "I think you'd better go in for a general checkup."

Wally's expression brightened. "You mean—you aren't going to tell . . ."

"Tell what?" Granthan demanded.

"About how I threatened to kill you—held a gun on you and all—"

"Had a bad dream, eh, Wally? I don't think the staff at the clinic has time for analyzing nightmares. Let's go."

11

The interview in the office of Flag-Captain Boyle, second in command aboard *Belshazzar,* twelve hours out of Terra on the trans-Plutonian run, was brief and to the point:

"I don't believe in this nonsense about mysterious voices inciting men to mutiny," the short, stocky officer told Granthan in a tone like a hundred-ton roller pulverizing gravel. "Sloppy discipline is more like it," he added. "No doubt there are a few malcontents stirring things up—that's nothing new. What's new is treating it as if it *were* new—giving official credence to these silly alibis. Well, you're here, and I'm a good enough Navy man to follow my orders, regardless of what I think of 'em. I won't get in your way—in fact I'll cooperate to the utmost. What do you want from me?"

"Nothing detrimental to shipboard routine or naval discipline, sir," Granthan replied reassuringly. "I just need to rig my detecting and recording devices as shown on the diagram. Your engineering officer has already given his technical approval—it won't interfere with normal ship functions."

Boyle glanced at the black-line print and tossed it aside. "What's the idea?" he grunted. "Listening devices in the heads, 3-V pickups in the mess, power station, armaments, and so on. All for what? Nothing to record there that isn't routine."

"I need data," Granthan pointed out. "If anything *does* happen, I want an objective record of it."

12

"Sure, I know all that stuff," Able Spaceman Spears said contemptuously. "Now get moving, Fats," he added, "before I decide to get rough."

CPO Victor Besosa, with forty years worth of service stripes on his sleeve and the pink-and-white of the Galactic Star leading off the five rows of ribbons on his chest, looked blankly at the recruit. Nothing in his experience had prepared him for this—it was like going to give a lettuce leaf to your pet bunny rabbit and having it go for your throat, he was thinking in a stunned way.

"Sure, kid, whatever you like," he heard himself say in a wheedling tone. "You want me to take your name off the duty roster, why, that's what I'll do. Just tell the log-room yeoman I said to scratch you for tonight. I'll fix up the paperwork later."

"Okay, now beat it, Fats," Spears snapped. "When I need you again, I'll let you know."

13

Granthan was sitting alone at a table in the officer's mess, half-consciously monitoring his consciousness

for signs of intrusion, while taking an occasional sip
from a mug of the black fluid known as "Navy coffee,"
actually an entirely nonorganic product of a Chinese
chemistry laboratory. It was part of the Navy's re-
venge, it was generally held, for being manned entirely
by the kind of jerk who'd volunteer for space duty.
He was watching a developing quarrel between two
young off-duty communications ensigns and three
slightly older computations officers who had seated
themselves with noisy joviality at the ensigns' table.
Granthan glanced up as someone brushed past his
back; he saw no one, turned to look in the other
direction. There was no one within fifty feet of him.
His faint irritation at being jostled evaporated, but he
frowned thoughtfully. His left hand, holding the coffee
mug, began to vibrate, ever so faintly. He concentrated
his attention on the tremor; it seemed to grow more
pronounced. He put down the heavy mug and spread
his fingers, watching them intently. His fingertips were
oscillating over an arc of about an eighth of an inch.
Then, without his willing it, his hand again clasped
the mug. He rose to his feet, cocked his arm, spilling
black Navy coffee down his sleeve, and pegged the
heavy container at the nearest of the noisy comput-
ermen.

"Belay that, bigmouth," he yelled, at the same time
watching, dispassionately, his amazing performance.
As he resumed his seat, the JG whom the mug had
struck jumped up with a yell; he took a wild swing
at a seated ensign, then turned on his fellow comp
men. The others grabbed him, all yelling at once.
None of them glanced toward Granthan. He closed
his eyes, willing out the din, and ran through a quick
mental exercise designed to impress on his conscious

recall every detail of the moment. Instead, he heard a shout:

NOT THIS ONE; IT IS TOO STRONG FOR US, MY MASTERS!

NONSENSE! SEIZE IT!

Astonished, Granthan thrust past the booming, silent voices, and groped in darkness. Reed would be amazed when he told him about this. Blake hadn't been exaggerating. He felt a tenuous pressure which seemed about to envelop him in an instantaneous spasm of panic: *Can't breathe!*

He pushed it aside, was falling, falling, endlessly, headlong. With an effort, he righted himself, slowed his fall, and was awake, lying on a hard cot. He sat up, saw the armed deck cop seated by the door of the small, iodoform-smelling room. The man glanced his way, his hand going to his holstered sidearm.

"Awake this time, mister?" he inquired. "Don't make a move. Just lay quiet. I got orders to shoot first and let the cap'n ask the questions later."

"What happened?" Granthan heard his voice croak. He coughed, tried again. "I remember being in the mess, and—and a fight started," he finished vaguely.

"You claiming you never pegged that mug at Mr. Clay?" the guard demanded without heat.

"No, I—" Granthan paused to think. "It was an accident; I mean—the voices—" He gave it up and found himself breathing as heavily as if he had just finished his daily ten-mile jog.

"Oh, another head case, eh?" the DP sneered. "Good a line as any, I guess," he added indifferently. "Come on. Cap'n wants to talk at you."

14

Captain Coign was a veteran of twenty-five years in space; nothing he had seen during that quarter-century had engraved any smile lines on his square-cut face. He looked at Granthan with no particular interest.

"You surprise me, mister," he commented, sounding unsurprised. "You came aboard my command with the highest recommendations; Captain Boyle gave you his okay, you kept quiet for two months, and last watch you went beserk. What's it all about?"

"I was posted here to investigate a phenomenon of the existence of which I was far from convinced, Captain," Granthan said quietly. "Last night—or whenever it was—I encountered it. Voices, just as reported, and motor interference as well. Not a hallucination; I've studied those—it was an actual input from outside my own mind. I don't remember what happened after that."

Coign grunted. "And those voices of yours told you to kill Mr. Clay," he suggested gently.

Granthan was startled. "Are you saying I committed murder, Captain?" he demanded.

The captain waved that away. "Not quite. He was still breathing when they pulled you off. You broke Chief Walters's nose," he added. "Walters was light heavyweight champion of the First Fleet back in 'twenty-three," he went on. "He's kind of pissed, being dumped by a civilian half his weight."

"That's unfortunate," Granthan said tightly. "The voices didn't tell me to do anything, just yammered at each other. The important thing is that now we know there's actually something out there."

"Oh, we do, eh?" Coign mused, almost smiling. "Well, what do we think it is? Just a big good-natured Voice that likes to stir things up?"

"It's an entity—or a group of entities—of fantastic mental power," Granthan said flatly. "And of no friendly disposition. I have to get back to my quarters, where I have equipment. I have to run this thing down. I can trace it—I think; maybe get some kind of handle on it."

"All right, all right. Don't get worked up, Mr. Granthan. You'll be returned to your quarters and permitted to tinker all you like. But any further disturbance and I'll brig you like any other troublemaker." He stood, a short, stocky figure in rumpled whites, his shoulder boards heavy with gold braid.

"Good luck in your research, sir," he said heavily. "Perhaps you'll come up with something that will mitigate the report I shall be forced to submit regarding this incident, but I doubt it."

15

Alone in the spartan cabin assigned to him, Granthan opened the large case he had prepared especially to enable him to continue his researches in space, at the closest possible range to the phenomena he hoped to examine. First he deployed a highly sensitive antenna of his own new and so far untested design. With it linked to a receiver also of his design, he hoped to detect the probing Gool thought-impulses before they crossed the threshold of human awareness. He consulted the rigging diagrams he had worked out for the apparatus, and after half an hour's work was ready for a trial. He made connections to an audio amplifier, and energized the system. He tuned carefully across the band where human mentation occurred, then activated the signal-seeking directional sniffer. At once, a Niagra-roar of white sound boomed out. Selectively, he filtered the reception, damping out broad spectra overwhelmed by star static, and refined the sensitivity of the receptor plates to those frequency-resonance patterns he had previously deduced for the phenomenon, based on theoretical considerations. At last a clear "voice" came through, an acoustic pattern he recognized as analogous to the intrusive "voices" by which he had been assailed in the mess.

—INTOLERABLE! LINK, MY MASTERS, FIND THE SOURCE OF THIS INTRUSION AND DESTROY IT!

ROUSE UP, MY MASTERS! ENOUGH OF SLOTH! THE HOUR IS AT HAND TO STRIKE OUT FOR [incomprehensible]. LONG HAVE WE BIDED OUR TIME. NOW INDEED [incomprehensible]. ACT AT ONCE!

His intensively trained language cortex, Granthan realized, was analyzing the alien sounds to their concept-content, and converting them to familiar equivalents. He played back the intercept at audio frequencies, this time hearing, from the recording, only a guttural snarling.

"I wonder," he muttered, half aloud, at the same

time reaching over to rearrange his jury-rigged antenna connections. Then, cautiously, feeling his way, he made a mental adjustment, from receive to transmit, furthur adjusted his apparatus, and, mimicking the alien "voice," sent:

"Forget it, boys. Go back to sleep, before you make me mad. Silence! Ignore this command at your peril."

At once, the Gool voice slammed at him, directly, booming inside his skull:

THIS INSOLENCE IS NOT TO BE TOLERATED, MY MASTERS. PINPOINT THIS ENTITY WHICH DARES TO INTRUDE, AND STRIKE HARD!

Holding the clear-cut, mind-to-mind contact, Granthan scanned it expertly, perceived its curious structure, saw that with a boost *here* and a slight realignment *there,* he could erect a trace which would enable him instantly to reestablish contact at will. Pausing only to flip the switches which would record the profile of the manifestation at the moment, Granthan switched off. He was badly shaken; he had acquired invaluable information no doubt, but at the cost, perhaps, of focusing the alien's attention on himself, and possibly thereby attracting some actively hostile action by the enigmatic Gool. Perhaps it had been a major blunder. Clearly, it was his responsibility to report the matter immediately to Captain Coign, and alert him to some possible attack. He felt a vague uneasiness; before he could move, the cold Gool voice slashed at him like a lash:

IMMOBILIZE THIS ONE. LATER WE WILL DISSECT IT AND LEARN ITS PETTY SECRETS.

IT IS BUT DIFFICULT, GREAT ONE. IT WRITHES UNDER MY TOUCH. IT ELUDES ME!

STRIKE NOW!

Granthan felt himself slammed backward by a disembodied blow. He struggled to retain his balance, felt the input slacken, but it did not fade entirely. A force more tenuous than cobwebs enveloped him, holding firm in spite of his most potent counterthrusts. Then he realized the magnitude of his blunder: while he had been preoccupied with tracing and consolidating his contact, the Gool had preempted his circuitry to direct its blow directly to his unprepared cortex. Now it gripped him in a seamless embrace, against which he could not even struggle. Sorry, Reed, he thought. They've won. Then in an instant the pressure was gone. Granthan reached tentatively, encountered no resistance.

With an effort as if he were forcing himself awake from a nightmare, Granthan struggled to his feet. He took a step and staggered, sick and dizzy. He reached the talker and slapped the TALK key.

"Captain, I must see you at once," he managed to say, blurrily, on the third try. Coign's bark of acknowledgment came at once:

"Not now, mister! Are you drunk? You sound—"

"Belay that, Captain," Granthan yelled. "I have to warn you—"

"You'd threaten me, you damned civilian egghead?" Coign yelled back. "I've got my hands full at the moment, Granthan, but I assure you that as soon as it's convenient I'll see to you. Now you're under arrest in quarters. I'm ordering my DPs to shoot you on sight!"

"Don't be a damned fool, Coign!" Granthan shouted in reply, but the talker was dead. He opened the door and stepped into the narrow passage. No one was in sight, but he could hear shouting in the distance, then two shots from a power pistol. A whiff of burned insulation came to his nostrils. He went quickly along to the lift serving the command levels. As he entered it a hard-shot *whang!*ed off the bulkhead inches away. He ignored it, and the yells that followed, punched in A-deck, and was whisked upward. He stepped out into a confusion of buzzing, clattering, clicking and electronic humming, not unmixed with curses delivered in Coign's gravelly tones.

"Stop there, mister, or I'll burn you myself!" the captain barked. He was standing with his back to the battle board, half of the dials on which were oscillating wildly, while the rest showed red "nonfunctional" lights. Coign's eyes were wild, but he was gripping his issue sidearm steadily, aimed squarely at Granthan's face. Granthan halted.

"What's this about, Captain?" he demanded coldly.

"You'd call *me* to an accounting, you damned traitor?" Coign almost screamed, and Granthan dropped to the floor in the same instant that the power pistol's ball-lightning bolt crackled through the space he had occupied a millisecond before, to bounce off the bulkhead and ricochet across the cramped compartment, dancing like St. Elmo's fire across the panel before winking out.

"You took me for a fool you could delude and use," Coign snarled. "I saw the power-demand you were drawing for a second or two before the panel fused," he amplified, almost calmly now. "Before I could cut you off at the knees the damage was done," he added, holstering his weapon. "But don't make the mistake of imagining you've won as easily as that. I have resources you don't know about, and I assure you that before I let you turn my command over to your infernal friends, the Gool, I'll scuttle her!" He lunged for a small, recently installed panel set into a corner of the main board. Granthan came to his feet and caught the officer's wrist, threw him aside and wrenched the auxiliary destruct panel from its mounting.

"Your trick didn't work!" Coign was yelling as he got to his feet. "Did you think I wouldn't notice that the power surge came at the same moment as your bogeyman sound effects?" He was facing Granthan now, saliva on his chin.

"'Voices,' eh?" he sneered. "Certainly, I heard your voices—*you,* hoking it up over the PA system. 'Link up, my masters,'" he intoned in a sepulchral voice. "Your childish pranks won't work here, mister! You're under arrest, and—" Coign broke off abruptly as a heavy tremor shook the deck underfoot. He lunged toward Granthan, who stepped aside.

"—and while my attention was diverted," the frantic captain shouted almost in Granthan's face, "your friends would attack my command unnoticed! Well, it didn't work!" Coign whirled and strode to the command talker.

"Hear this," he yelled. "Condition red! All hands to action stations, Security mode two! This vessel is under attack. Ignore any apparent instructions not in accordance with this order! Repeat! Action stations. Stand by to repel boarders."

"You're wasting your time, Captain," Granthan said quietly. "If you'll calm yourself and allow me to study the situation, perhaps I can do something."

"Haven't you done enough?" Coign demanded.

"You've leapt to an erroneous conclusion, sir," Granthan assured the excited captain calmly, as the ship shuddered again.

"Are you trying to say this has nothing to do with you?" Coign yelled, clutching for the support as the deck took on a decided list astern.

"I may inadvertently have attracted Gool attention to us," Granthan told the frantic officer. "But I have some ideas—"

"Damn you and your ideas!" Coign screamed, retaining his footing with difficulty as the slow tilting of the deck halted with a heavy shock. He reached for a handhold, struggled across to the arms locker beside the main panel, wrenched a crater gun from its clip, and fired wildly at Granthan. Now, suddenly, sounds of pandemonium were audible beyond the hatch.

"You're making a mistake, Captain," Granthan said quietly but firmly over the background hubbub. "At this moment," he went on steadily, "I'm your only chance. Don't blow it. I'm here precisely to deal with an incident such as now appears to be in progress. Just be quiet now, and let me think."

"I'll let daylight through you, damn you!" Coign yelped and fired and missed again, scoring the bulkhead beside Granthan, who stepped in quickly, caught the hot barrel of the weapon, and wrenched it from Coign's grip. He tossed it aside.

"We won't be needing that, Captain," he said, his face an inch from the officer's. "I don't know what's happening here, but it's not an attempt to board, I'm sure of that. Now get it together and tell your crew to stand easy, and await your orders. They're rioting out there." He nodded toward the hatch. "By the way," he added quietly, "you might take a look at the accelerometer."

As if against his will, Coign glanced at the complex digital array which registered all movement of the great space vessel. It was blank.

"It's blown," he grated. "How did you know—"

"It's functioning perfectly, Captain," Granthan assured the shaken officer. "Believe it. The ship is at rest."

Coign stared at him wildly as another shudder shook the deck. "At rest, is it?" he yelled, a yell which slipped into a yelp as the deck tilted sharply. Granthan caught the captain's arm and steadied him. "The vessel is at rest," he repeated. "We just *think* it's bouncing around. Notice, now." He took a coin from his pocket and balanced it on edge on the chart table. A heavy shock rocked the ship, but the coin remained upright.

"This is not the time for magic tricks, Granthan," Coign blurted, tears in his eyes.

"It's an illusion, Captain," Granthan explained tightly. "It's the Gool-mind, making you think you're under bombardment or worse. I've stopped believing in it, so I don't notice it anymore. Now, get on the talker and tell the men to stand easy, before somebody does something foolish."

"You admit you're in communication with the enemy," Coign said brokenly. "Now you're trying to talk me into surrendering. Well, it won't work, damn you!" He wrenched his arm free of Granthan's grip and wiped at his eyes with his callused knuckles.

NOT SUFFICIENT, MY MASTERS! the sepulchral Gool

voice boomed out abruptly. THE PERVERSE ONE RE-
SISTS. LINK UP!

"That *can't* be you," Coign stammered. "Unless
you recorded it before. But what—?"

"Stop trying to make me the heavy," Granthan said,
feeling weary. "Do you notice the buffeting has
stopped?"

Without answering, Coign groped blindly to the
command talker and called, "Hear this!" Then, "As
you were," he ordered, his voice firm. "This has been
an exercise, testing my alert system," he went on.
"Back to duty stations, men, the alert is canceled."
He looked at Granthan warily. "I don't know what in
the Nine Hells is going on here, Granthan. Do you
think you can explain it to me?"

"We're up against an entity, or entities of some
kind, of enormous mental power," Granthan said.
"Power they can channel, and use to play with our
minds—even manipulate matter, I think. We have to
be on guard at every moment—" He broke off as the
deck slanted underfoot, grabbed for support as the tilt
increased. Coign had a wild look on his face as he
lunged for Granthan.

"Tricky, aren't you, boy!" the officer yelled as
Granthan caught his wrists, holding him off. "You
almost had me convinced you were in the clear, but
you—but, why?"

"Not me," Granthan said tightly. "More Gool
tricks—"

"That line worked once, Granthan," Coign grated,
his face looking greenish-pale. "But you goofed. Why
didn't you hold off for a few more seconds? I'd have
been sending you on your way to raise hell un-
impeded!"

"Because I've got nothing to do with this," Granthan repeated tiredly. "And if I'm raising hell around here, you don't seem to be impeding me much. Get hold of yourself, Captain: take a look at the chart table."

Coign's gaze shifted briefly from Granthan's face to the lighted table, littered with scales, light-scribes, and pointers. Abruptly he backed off, and Granthan released his hold; at once, Coign retched, staggering, almost fell.

"They're not sliding," Coign said brokenly, as he struggled to his feet. "So the floor's not really at forty-five degrees and precessing." He gulped. "But I'm seasick as a drunken Middie." He was studying the floor as if willing it to remain horizontal, still frantically clutching a stanchion.

"It's all right, Captain. Just your semicircular canals responding to the idea you're rocking sideways. Now that you realize it's an illusion, you should be able to reorient yourself. The deck is flat and stationary. Go ahead, plant your feet and let go that grabhandle; you won't fall."

The talker crackled and boomed out: "Captain, this is Chief Warfield, Power Section. We got a fire in here like a haystack burning. Funny thing, it's right on the open deck, where there's nothing inflammable. Sprinkler system's out, too. I got the men out, and I'm going to try the manual damping system before I abandon post. What are your orders, sir? Hot in here . . ." His voice trailed off.

"As you were, Warfield," Granthan ordered curtly.

"There's no fire, Chief," Coign took over, speaking steadily into the talker linked to Power Section. "Cut out, if you're hot, and cool off, but don't foam the compartment! Got that, Chief?"

"It's Space'n Second Brown, Cap'n," another voice came in. "Chief's out cold. Musta went nuts, yelling about a fire and all. No fire here, like you said. Send the corpsmen, please, sir."

"Now, you listen to me, Brown," the captain growled, his face an inch from the talker. "You take care of Warfield the best way you can until I can get some help down there. Stay at your post no matter what! Keep Power Section functioning. Clear?"

"Yessir, I'll do my best, sir," Brown's voice came back without conviction.

"Someone's trying to hoax us, Brown," Coign said urgently. "We've got to hold on. I'm counting on you, Spaceman First Brown."

"Second, sir," Brown corrected. "No promo in six years in the Fleet."

"I said 'First,'" Coign growled. "Carry on." He looked warily at Granthan. The deck seemed steady underfoot now.

"What next, mister?" he demanded.

"Is it understood now, Captain, that this is no damn-fool joke of mine?" Granthan returned.

Coign nodded reluctantly. "Don't know what it is," he acknowledged. "But I guess it's not your doing, unless you're some kind of magician. But what do we do now?"

"That's a lot better, Captain," Granthan said. "If we can work together, maybe we can handle this."

"But what's it all *for*?" Coign almost wailed. "What good's it going to do these ghouls or whatever to make us think the ship's tumbling?"

"That's easy, Captain," Granthan replied. "If *we* go ape and wreck the ship, *they* don't have to lift a pseudopod."

"Hell of a thing this had to happen aboard *my* command," Coign muttered. "I'm on record as saying all this ghoul business is some publicity hound's idea of a way to sell a few hours of airtime. Look like a fool."

"How you look is the least of our concerns at the moment, Coign," Granthan said harshly. "Right now you'd better get on the squawk box and tell the men what's happened—no more bedtime stories about drills. Let 'em know they've been deluded—almost as if we had a hypnotic gas in the ship, made everybody see things."

Coign nodded curtly. "Now hear this," he commanded. "This is the captain speaking. All hands— men, we've been gassed and having hallucinations; we're in the clear for the moment, but it could hit again. If so, just stick to your normal ship's routine. Ignore anything unusual."

"That should stabilize matters for the moment," Granthan approved. Before Coign could reply, the compartment door burst open and a burly man in work-stained whites with the six stripes of a superchief slammed into the sacrosanct COC. In one fist he held a service pistol which he aimed without hesitation at Coign.

"I heard that, Captain," he said in the high-pitched tones of incipient hysteria. "'Everything's jake' is it? 'Ignore anything unusual.' Hell's bells, and me watching the black gribbles coming out of the bulkhead by the zillion. I see they've got to you, Cap'n—but Superchief Bonzano's still got his marbles intact. So I'm taking 'immediate, effective action,' just like Navy regs say." He took another step toward Coign, ignoring Granthan, who saw the big fellow's finger tight-

ening on the firing stud. With a casual motion,
Granthan reached across the plotting table, picked up
a steel-edged meter rule, still standard issue on naval
vessels more as a tribute to tradition than as a practical
navigational aid. He brought the heavy rule over in a
whistling arc to impact against Bonzano's thick forearm. The gun clattered to the deck, and Coign stepped
in fast and kicked it away. The big man stumbled back
with a yell.

Coign followed him closely. "Just calm yourself,
man," he commanded. "I'll take care of the gribbles."
He turned to the talker and ordered up a brace of deck
police to take the fellow away.

"Out of his mind," he explained aloud to himself.
"Man's got twenty-eight years service and a Cross,
Second Class. He'll be all right." Coign turned to
Granthan.

"I suppose this is where I apologize, mister, and
give you a free hand," he growled. "Not bloody likely."
He shook his head and snorted as if attempting to
dispel a stench. "You probably staged the whole incident—if there *was* an incident. Made a damn fool
of me."

"We've got to start believing our senses at some
point, Captain," Granthan countered. "A good start
would be to cancel the kill order on me and let me
get back to work. I came up here to let you know I
was working on it and not to panic. That's still my
advice."

"Panic, eh?" Coign sneered. "That'll be a hot day
at South Polar Dome, *civilian!* Now get out of here
and do what you can. Don't worry, I'll tell 'em to let
you through."

"Thanks for nothing much," Granthan replied indifferently. "Don't call me; I'll call you, *sir.*"

Coign was busy at the table as Granthan left the cramped COC. In the passage, aside from odors of burning, everything appeared normal. He set off at a fast walk toward his quarters in the storage area.

16

Two men were waiting by his door. They were a couple of perennial space'n last class from the Cargo Section, Granthan saw: they elaborately failed to notice him until he stepped between them and reached for the latch. Then they turned in awkward synchronization and reached. Granthan broke the elbow of the bigger of the two, and power-kicked the kneecap, shin, and arch of the other. They collapsed on each other, howling in pain, as Granthan slid inside and secured the latch. Somewhat to his surprise, there was no one awaiting him, but the cramped chamber had been ransacked; the complex antenna had been partially ripped down and trampled underfoot. A soiled sheet of brown wrapping paper lay amid the ruins. On it was scrawled in red crayon: WE KILL TRAITORS.

Granthan picked his way across the litter to the modified field-model control panel he had erected. As he reached it, he was surprised to see readings in the blue on all three scales which registered aspects of field intensity. At the same moment, the silent voice (or voices, he was unsure which) boomed out with unexampled clarity:

LINK, BROTHERS, WITH PRECISION. CLEARLY, THE
CRUDE DIRECT APPROACH IS INEFFECTIVE. HENCE, WE
MUST EMPLOY SUBTLETY, THUS—

"Wait a minute," Granthan muttered aloud, to himself, tracing with practiced eye the tangled elements
of his antenna. With a sudden shock of excitement he
realized what had happened; by sheerest accident, the
array had been so modified as to cut out of the circuit
an entire segment of the amplification structure, tying
the main sensor directly to the fine-focus elements.
The result, astoundingly, was a vast improvement in
his reception. At once, Granthan introspected, noting
how the minute subliminal signal now impinged directly on his self-awareness field. And if he traced
the signal back, with infinite caution, he could deduce
a pattern here; he could conceptualize a path of perme-
ability *there*—

GET OUT!

The mental impulse hurled him back, his muscles
in spasm. His skull seemed to ring with the aftershock
of the blast of mentational energy his unsuspecting
mind had taken. The voice raged on:

INTOLERABLE! DESTROY IT—YET HOLD, BROTHERS.
PERHAPS—the powerful voice trailed off into a hubbub
of question-and-answer. Dazed, Granthan withdrew
from contact, set about tidying the ravaged cabin, his
mind dwelling on the intricate structure of intangibility
he had glimpsed. Perhaps, he thought excitedly, if I
marshal my resources, apply pressure at that node,
then *thrust*. . . . His concept, clearly glimpsed for only
an instant, faded.

As he relinquished contact, Granthan sensed the
activity of the Gool-mind, no longer directed at him,

but intent on some complex task; then it was gone. What, he wondered, are they up to now?

Mastering himself, Granthan applied all of his highly trained intellect to the task of analyzing what he had observed, straining to capture the elusive and vastly exciting possibility which seemed to hover at the edge of his awareness. He was still engrossed in the task when the bulkhead collapsed, the deck buckling underfoot, knocking him down. Fire raged at him, a gigantic impact of heat and pressure. He felt himself lifted, thrown back. The air seemed to sear his lungs. The pressures were intolerable. Surely his bones would break. Agony blanked out thought, except for the realization that came with shocking finality: The ship was breaking up.

CHAPTER TWO

1

Out of chaos, Granthan groped his way back to awareness. He was drifting in space amid shattered fragments of metal and synthetics. He made a tentative movement which set him to spinning slowly about his long axis. A fragment of three-inch-thick structural alloy floated by, its edges broken clean. The stern admonition NO SMOKING was stenciled across the gray surface. Granthan recognized it as a piece of the passage just outside his cabin door.

"But that's nonsense," he said aloud, but the utter silence was unbroken. "If I were exposed to space, I'd have exploded and the remains would be frozen; I wouldn't be lying around thinking up snappy comebacks to notices painted on what used to be the bulkhead. And I certainly wouldn't be talking to myself and listening carefully to the answers.

"So," he reflected without urgency, "I'm not really

where I think I am. This is another piece of Gool sleight of hand. I'm still in my quarters, and the ship is still intact." On that thought, consciousness faded.

The next time Granthan awoke, he was lying on the deck beside the case containing his test gear. He got to his feet, finding everything functional, briefly recalled the adrift-in-space episode, and dismissed it. Or almost. Even as he thrust the illusion aside, he noticed how cleverly it had been insinuated among the laminae of his world-concept, scrupulously complying with the contours of his preconceptions. All except one, he noted with a sense of triumph.

"You're great psychologists," he said aloud, and this time he heard his own words.

"But not *quite* as good as you think you are, Mr. Gool. You forgot one little item: I don't conceive of myself as dead, or even dying. I don't accept losing, so your illusion rings as phony as an SBA dollar." Now, Granthan told himself sternly, it's time to stop indulging myself and get to work on the problem. Which is—he hesitated. I'm under attack by an entity, perhaps a compound entity, which is capable of manipulating my awareness field to create illusions. Illusions can't hurt me unless I act on them, so the first step is to sit tight and figure the thing out. This kind of long-range control implies fantastically tightly beamed energies in the omega range, well beyond native human abilities, but not totally unrelated thereto. I can use as a working hypothesis Müller's idea that we're dealing with a repeating spectrum, like visible light: starts and ends with red; if we could see higher and lower in the electromagnetic spectrum, we'd see all the colors repeat. So the analog to omega in this scheme would be good old alpha. Now let's take a look at the Gool at alpha.

Granthan was shocked by the sudden insurge of visualization—a rush of vivid images which sent him reeling back—but only for a moment. Then he was able to compartmentalize the alien impressions, distance himself therefrom, and study them:

"Definitely a compound mind, not as totally synchronized as is theoretically possible, and thus vulnerable to the right kind of counterthrust, if..."—Granthan paused to consider—"if I can design the proper riposte."

As Granthan hesitated, wrestling inwardly with the fantastically complex problem confronting him, he became subliminally aware of sounds from beyond the cramped compartment: sounds of combat: gunfire, shouts: Coign! Left alone, no doubt the outraged commander had set out to handle matters in his own way. With Big Joe Bonzano on the loose, beset by black gribbles...

Granthan paused to buckle on the sidearm which had been issued to him at Navy HQ—not without an all-encompassing caution against actually using it, he recalled wryly, as he ejected the power cell and dropped it into his pocket. Nevertheless, the weight of the weapon on his hip was comforting as he stepped out into the din of riot near at hand. The stink of burning synthetics, mixed with the pungent odors of energy-weapon discharges, was thick in the air, and accompanied by a drifting stratum of blackish smoke at head level. Granthan snorted it from his nose and went along quietly to the cross-corridor. Bonzano stood ten feet away, his back to Granthan, aiming a pistol that was the twin of the one at Granthan's hip—but aimed at what, Granthan could not see. Then he heard Coign's gravelly voice, not as rock-steady as usual, but far from hysteria:

"I'm telling you for the final time, mister, drop it now, and at your court martial extenuating circumstances will be taken into consideration."

"They're deeper every second," the big noncom yelled back. "Coming out and crawling down and piling up. Up to my knees now, damn near—and you're giving me the old guff about ship punishment—as if you had anything to say about it anymore . . . sir."

Granthan moved up silently; Coign's expression showed not a flicker as his eyes fell on Granthan and moved on. Bonzano shifted position to lean against the bulkhead; as if casually Granthan rammed his pistol's muzzle firmly into the big NCO's neck. Bonzano went rigid.

"Drop it, Joe," Granthan ordered. Bonzano ignored him.

"This is against your third cervical vertebra," Granthan said quietly. "If you should happen to survive the loss of blood and the untreated shock, you're still not the type to spend the rest of your life happily in a float-chair with an autopan." There was still no reaction from Bonzano. Coign watched silently, with an expression of mild interest.

"Use your head, Bonzano," Granthan suggested in a reasonable tone. "We're under attack by an enemy that can play with our minds. It can't hurt us; it can only make us hurt each other. Your black gribbles are imaginary, you know, Joe."

"I know what I see," Bonzano replied doggedly.

"Be reasonable," Granthan urged. "Consider; what would it take to pierce that bulkhead?"

"A number-three penetrating could do it," Bonzano answered. "Maybe."

"And these gribbles of yours," Granthan prodded. "Describe them."

"Like caterpillars," Bonzano said promptly. "Black; shiny, like they was wet; sort of jelly, you know."

"Now think, Joe," Granthan said urgently. "Could a soft worm burrow through that flint-steel?"

"Not on your life," Bonzano responded. "Don't know how they do it."

"The answer is they don't do it," Granthan told the big fellow. "You're under attack, Joe. The attack is a form of telepathic hypnosis; it makes you think you see things that aren't there. Don't let the Gool make a fool of you. You know better."

"Damn right," Bonzano said, and let the weapon drop. He turned carefully and said, "I figured it was you, Mr. Granthan. What's the idea? Seems like I heard you having a set-to with the captain yourself a few minutes ago. Why are you siding with him now?"

"I promised to write 'I will not sass the captain' a hundred times on the blackboard, so he let me off," Granthan said seriously.

"Funny thing," Bonzano said casually. "The gribbles is gone. All of 'em. I can see the deck. How'd you do that, Mr. Granthan? You must have something on the ball after all." He lowered the issue weapon and holstered it carefully.

"What's the rioting all about, Chief?" Coign asked the big fellow.

"Well, lots of things, Cap'n," Bonzano replied thoughtfully. "There's Harry Thompson, got big yellow butterflies all over him—and Jersey Tom Jones— he says we been boarded by a bunch of bright-green skeletons, glows in the dark, he says. I'm beginning to get the sketch." Bonzano went on, thinking aloud: "No two guys can agree on what the problem is— but it seems like they've sort of shaped up into two parties: them that want to blow up the ship, and them that mean to stop 'em. They're all as messed up in the head as I was—thanks, Mr. Granthan, for straightening me out. But how you going to get Warfield and Big Jim Walcott and some of them boys to sit still for you?"

"I'm counting on you for that, Joe," Granthan said. "Go out there and restore some order."

Bonzano nodded gravely. "I'll do what I can. Permission to return to my duty station, Cap'n, sir."

Coign gravely returned the man's salute. "Carry on, Chief," he said. "Try not to shoot anyone unless there's no other way."

Bonzano about-faced and went out into the clamor of the passageway.

"You handled that very nicely, Mr. Granthan," Coign said. "I owe you an apology," he added in a tone that suggested it might be some time before he paid. "Now what do you advise?"

"I suggest we try to stay alive until you can get control of the bridge, sir," Granthan said earnestly. "And if you see anything impossible, or even highly unlikely, don't believe it. We can fight these Gool and win, Captain."

"Wait a minute, Mr. Granthan," Coign said abruptly.

"How do I know *you're* not a hallucination, designed to con me into doing the wrong thing?"

"We have to start somewhere, Captain," Granthan pointed out. "I find that I accept you—and Chief Bonzano too—without a doubt in the world. Yet, of course, you *could* be an illusion. Well, I say we take this as our starting point, and keep our eyes open for any telltale discrepancies."

"I suppose that's all we *can* do," Coign agreed. "Now let's get to the bridge and see how much damage has been done there by crew fighting black gribbles." He turned and set off briskly along the littered passage and Granthan followed.

2

The gang was lying in wait at the lift vestibule, six men with weapons which included an officer's model Mark X and a pry-bar from Cargo Section. Most had untreated wounds, and several were busily batting ineffectually at invisible harassers. The leader apparently was the man whose elbow Granthan had broken. The arm was in an improvised sling. He advanced on Granthan, ignoring the captain.

"Well, look what we got here," he said to no one in particular, in the tone of a schoolyard bully. Granthan returned the man's sneering gaze calmly.

"Just what do *you* think you have here, Gunderson?" Granthan inquired in an interested tone. "For the sake of your future career, if you have one, you'd do well to snap to and await your captain's instructions." As he spoke, Granthan shifted slightly to the left so that when Gunderson's left fist lashed out, he leaned easily aside and took the arm in a firm grip, levering the elbow backward over his forearm. "You're about to run out of arms, Gus," Granthan said in a casual tone as he increased the pressure, bringing the heavyset cargo handler to his toes.

"Leave go my arm, wise guy," Gunderson grated past clenched teeth. "Before I..." His threat faded out and he twisted away, in an attempt to relieve the pressure of his tormented arm. Granthan increased the leverage sharply. Gunderson yelped and tried to back away.

"Better give up trying to be a tough guy, Gus," Granthan advised in a kindly tone. "You're not very good at it. By the way, what's your beef?" He eased off the pressure, slightly, retaining his grip.

"Just ask Warfield," the now limp and sobbing man gasped. "He'll tell you."

Warfield separated himself from the gang and stepped forward, as Granthan released Gunderson and pushed him away.

"What's the idea, Mr. Dirtcrawler?" Warfield demanded, with a quick glance at Captain Coign, who was standing at Granthan's side looking grim.

"The idea, Chief," Granthan replied, "is that you'd better decide quick whether you want to blow up your ship or help those who are trying to save her."

"I never said—" Warfield started and cut himself off. "I don't hafta answer to no *civilian*," he amended.

"Yeah?" the bass voice of Joe Bonzano sounded off as the big fellow thrust up beside Warfield. "How about me, rookie?" He pushed his face close to Warfield, who tried to avert his eyes. "You telling *me* you don't hafta take orders, Mr. Warfield?" Bonzano almost yelled.

"Now, Joe, take it easy—" Warfield countered, retiring behind Granthan.

"Don't tell *me* when to take it easy," Bonzano replied, grabbing Warfield's arm. "What are you doing away from your duty station? I hear you're putting out some dumb story about a haystack on fire in Power Section!"

"I never said nothing about no haystack!" Warfield almost wailed. "Why you jumping on me, Joe?"

"That's *Chief* Bonzano to you, short-timer," Bonzano barked at the rapidly wilting Power Section veteran. "You let garbage pile up in your section until you had enough for a bonfire, that it?" the senior noncom yelled in Warfield's face, his fist hovering nearby on call.

"You know better'n that, Chief," Warfield objected. "I run a tight section. I got six Navy Es in the last twelve years."

"And now you're trying for a big M for mutiny, is that it? Come on, Max," Bonzano said in a more kindly tone. "You been had, boy."

"I guess I know a fire when I see one," Warfield grumbled, as he backed away.

"Is that right, mister?" Bonzano said sarcastically. "What's the kindling temperature of them deck plates?"

Warfield looked startled. "That's Class Four W hardplate," he said defensively. "Might get combustion in pure oxy at a little over three thousand F."

"So that kind of leaves out the idea that it just sort

of ignited spontaneously, Max," Bonzano pointed out, his words clearly audible to all the men above the much diminished clamor. "You didn't leave no hay-stack laying around, and the vessel won't burn too good by itself in ship air, so—use your head, Max. If you was a first-hitch greeny, maybe I could see it; but I always thought you had twenty years in Power. So knock off the crap!"

"All right," Warfield came back with more assur-ance. "Then what did I see burning? Smelled it, too," he added. "And I mean it was *hot*."

"Okay," Bonzano said wearily. "If you can see a fire that ain't there, I guess you could smell it, feel it, too. So you're smelling things, Max. Like Mr. Granthan told us before, these here Gool can mix up a fellow's brain so he sees stuff that ain't there. Now, are you on your way back to station, or do I hafta deal with Acting Chief Brown?"

"I was just going, Joe—uh, I mean Chief Bonzano," Warfield blurted, pushing through his now silent fel-lows, some of whom peeled off to follow him as he hurried away. The others drifted off.

"Starting now," Coign called after the cowed men, "it goes in the record. Now, let's put this vessel in a condition of readiness." He turned to Bonzano.

"You did that just right, Joe," he said quietly. "You, too, Granthan," he added. "Now I think our problems are over."

"Not necessarily, Captain," Granthan put in, equally *sotto voce*. "I suggest we go directly to the bridge and get set for the next move. The Gool aren't through yet."

"They did their damnedest and lost," Coign objected. "It didn't work, so now I shall write up my report of this incident—and you may be assured you'll receive favorable mention, sir—and get on with my duties."

As they talked, the two men had moved along to the wardroom. Coign paused.

"Coffee, Mr. Granthan?" he invited.

"I think I'd better get back to my quarters, sir," Granthan declined gravely, "and see if I can get a line on what's likely to happen next."

"I said forget it, Granthan!" Coign barked. "I'm still master aboard this vessel, and I want this foolish incident forgotten as soon as possible. I *don't* want an outsider keeping it alive by poking around after order's been restored!"

"If order has been restored, Captain," Granthan resisted. "We've dealt with one bunch; there may well be others."

"Very well," Coign grumped. "You go your way; I shall see to my ship." He walked away. A moment later, Granthan, who had started in the opposite direction, heard a hoarse yell behind him. He went flat against the wall and looked back. A man staggered into view, his face bloody. Coign recognized Brown, the level-headed number two in Power Section. The battered man saw Granthan and came toward him at a run. As Granthan stepped forward to meet him, Brown halted abruptly to wipe at his bleeding nose.

"What happened to you, Brown?" Granthan inquired.

"Nothing," the powerman answered shortly. He stood eyeing Granthan speculatively. Suddenly, Granthan stepped forward, jerked the handgun from

Brown's waistband and threw it behind him.

"Hey—what's . . . ?" Brown started to bluster.

"I'm a mind reader," Granthan said shortly.

"Won't do you any good," Brown said in a dull voice. "Over three hundred to one: nobody can buck those odds." Then he launched himself at but past Granthan, diving for the gun. Granthan deflected him with a thrust and picked up the weapon. Brown lunged again, this time directly at Granthan's throat, but met instead a hard fist; he collapsed, groaning and fingering his already bruised face.

"What's the idea, Brown?" Granthan demanded. "I thought you were a loyal spaceman."

Brown looked up at him with pain-filled eyes. "Cap'n's orders," he said shortly, and got to his feet, watching Granthan warily.

"I doubt that, Brown," Granthan said quietly.

"You'd be wrong, mister," Coign's voice spoke harshly behind Granthan. He turned to see the captain standing flat-footed, holding his heavy power gun aimed steadily.

"I understood we had an agreement, Captain," Granthan said mildly. "What do you expect to accomplish by shooting me now?"

"I took your advice, Professor," Coign came back harshly. "I started looking for the unlikely, the element that didn't fit—*you.*" He smiled the faintest of smiles. "A damned civilian aboard my command, in Deep Space, under condition red, and telling *me* what to do? Not very damned likely, Mr. Granthan. I'm master aboard this vessel, and I shall remain so. Now, Brown, move in carefully and take your piece—and *his* sidearm, too. You're lucky, Granthan," he went on.

"I've decided to brig you and take you in, instead of shooting you on the spot."

"Listen, Captain," Granthan suggested, handing the pistol to Brown, who took it and ducked back. "The ship's quiet. We've almost got things under control. I think we've got the Gool off-balance: things aren't going precisely as they intended. If I get back to my hutch quickly, I may be able to devise a counterattack before they decide on their next move." He took a step and the power gun, rock-steady in Coign's fist, scarred the bulkhead six inches from his ribs.

"You're damned right things are under control, mister," Coign rasped, "and they're going to stay that way. Now get moving. The brig's aft." He pointed along the passage. "Stay clear of him, Brown," he ordered the awed enlisted man.

"Don't be a damned fool, Brown," Granthan said almost casually. "You know as well as the captain does that I was assigned duties aboard this ship by Admiral-General Titus personally. There's no way I could have gotten aboard otherwise. Use your head, the captain is making a serious mistake: it's your duty not to let him."

"Shut up!" Coign yelled, and fired again, this time smashing Granthan back against the bulkhead; his knees buckled and he fell heavily, blood and smoke coming from a blackened wound in his left shoulder. Brown darted in and bent over the fallen Granthan, whose eyes opened and held Brown's.

"Stop him, Brown," Granthan gasped. "Save your ship and your shipmates and yourself. You have my Mark III. Take his away from him." His eyes closed and he went slack. Brown looked across at his captain.

"Sir, you can't just shoot a man down like a dog!" he managed, in a choked voice. "You're in command, Captain Coign, and I'm only a Space'n Second, but there's no regulation says you can kill people!"

"Just calm yourself, Spaceman," Coign replied calmly. "In any case, I shot to disable the fool, not to kill him. It's not your responsibility."

"I guess it is, sir," Brown mumbled and dived toward the captain, hands outstretched for the heavy handgun. It uttered its harsh croak again, and Brown folded in mid-leap, struck the deck limply and lay moving feebly.

"You've shot a good man, Coign," Granthan said, struggling to sit up. "I'm going to my quarters now, and if you're ready for another murder, you can stop me." He came to his feet as Coign approached warily, his gun aimed unwaveringly at Granthan's face.

"Next time," the haggard-faced officer grated, "I won't shoot to wound."

"You won't shoot at all, sucker," Granthan said clearly, and spun sideways. Coign swiveled to keep him covered, but did not fire.

"You move fast for a fellow with a hole the size of my fist burned in his arm," the captain snarled. "But it won't help you. I'm not quite the sucker you imagine." Granthan saw the captain's finger begin to tighten on the firing stud; he closed his eyes to shut out distraction, and concentrated on the mnemonic which would trigger the posthypnotic suggestion he had imprinted much earlier, in preparation for some unforeseen emergency. Now the emergency was at hand. He had, he estimated, two seconds, unless the drill worked. . . .

Abruptly, he bent double and hurled himself directly at Coign. The gun blast cracked harmlessly above him. At that moment, Brown, bleeding but ambulatory, rushed in and grappled Coign's gun arm with both hands. Coign threw him aside effortlessly, as Granthan slammed into him. The gun clattered on the floor, and Brown, one hand clamped over the wound in his side, recovered it, stood nervously covering both men, still locked together, Coign straining, Granthan holding the burly officer impotent.

"Captain, sir," Brown said uncertainly, "I'm no mutineer, but we've got to hear what Mr. Granthan's trying to tell us. Go ahead, Mr. Granthan."

"Shoot the traitor," Coign snapped. "That's a direct order, damn you, Brown!"

"No, sir," Brown replied firmly. "Better speak up, Mr. Granthan, while you got the chance."

"Very well, Spaceman," Granthan said. "Now, the situation seems to be stabilized for the moment. By breaking the Gool's lock on Bonzano and a few others, we've confused them; they're rethinking their tactics. But we can be sure they'll hit us again. Right now, I don't hear any rioting going on—but that could change at any moment. We have to work fast and carefully, and all of us have to keep alert for any sort of interference." Granthan stepped back, releasing Coign, who gave him a venomous look, and stood silent, rubbing his wrist. He glanced at Brown, who was pale and sweaty from loss of blood, but standing firm.

"Hand me that sidearm, Spaceman," Coign said as if absently, and held out his hand. Brown lowered the weapon and reversed it, but instead of passing it to his captain, he offered it to Granthan, who took it and thrust it into his belt.

"We can't waste any more time with nonsense,"

he said. "Now, Brown, you'd better get back to Power Section, just to be sure Warfield is tracking properly now. Captain, you and I will return to Command Deck, and take the appropriate action."

Coign nodded curtly. "I need to check out this command from one end to the other," he stated flatly. "I can do that via the monitor panels topside." He turned and walked away.

"I better find Space'n Cohn and get him to fix up that arm, Mr. Granthan," Brown said. "I'll check on the chief first, like you said, and then get back to you. Where'll you be, sir?"

"In my quarters," Granthan said. "Better make it fast," he added, his voice blurry now. "I can't fight it off much longer." He felt the deck tilt underfoot, realized he was leaning, and barely managed to retain his balance.

GO TO COMMAND DECK, the silent voice boomed. YOU MUST BE QUICK. YOU ARE DYING, STRANGELIFE. MAKE HASTE. YOU WILL RECEIVE FURTHUR INSTRUCTIONS. REMEMBER THAT ABOVE ALL, THE GREAT RACE MUST SURVIVE TO DOMINATE ALL. GO.

"Mr. Granthan, you going to be all right?" Brown's voice came, faintly, as from a great distance. Granthan blinked, could barely make out the young fellow's worried face, peering from a dense fog.

"Nope," he replied. "Get me to my quarters, Brown." He wanted to say more, but his strength was gone. Time to activate the second line of defense: another Personality Fraction, at a deeper level, able to dominate the autonomic nervous system. . . .

"Mr. Granthan?" Brown's voice echoed from an infinite distance. "You won't go and die on me now, Mr. Granthan? Please."

3

Granthan lay on his bunk, aware of the effort of breathing. Briefly, he wondered why he was bothering with the laborious business of hauling on the diaphragmatic arch, thus expanding the spongy lungs and reducing gas pressure within the manifold interconnected passages and alveoli, causing the higher-pressure ambient air to rush in to inflate the organs; then equally laboriously, pushing it out again. . . .

Then he forgot the problem and wondered instead why the voice urged him to AWAKE! ARISE! It went on to say that he was chosen to serve the Great Race and thus must not die. DO NOT DIE, STRANGELIFE! it yelled silently. Obediently, Granthan suppressed the shock syndrome, pinched off the broken blood vessels to the wound site, dragged in yet another breath, and another, endlessly laboring. For what? Yet that much was simple: so as to regain the perfection which had so unfairly been taken from him, the perfect peace, unflawed comfort. . . .

"Reexperiencing the birth trauma," Granthan muttered aloud. "Swell, I must be alive." He reached up and delicately investigated his wound with his fingertips. "About eight ounces of tissue destroyed, for openers," he told himself. "I must be some tough son of a bitch to be awake and thinking about it." But then of course the Great Race expected that he would not fail. "Up, Granthan, I saye and I doe," he intoned aloud, and was standing up looking at a curiously truncated, subtly *wrong* arrangement of wires webbed across the other end of the tiny chamber. Without conscious volition, he went across to it, adjusted the *yilk* axis, quickly aligned properly the *balve* grid, stripped away the superfluous parasitic members, closed the *fang* cycle, then relaxed his mind and allowed his *darm* energies to flow out, embrace the impalpable structure which pulsed around the now correctly integrated *vor* pattern. Freedom! Hastily he thrust aside the encumbering misconceptions which had inhibited him, and allowed his *darm* energies to fall effortlessly toward the leashed potencies of the Great Ones. He listened as they/it ruminated, communing with itself:

. . . WHEN WE/I HAVE EMPLOYED THIS TOOL CORRECTLY, IT WILL GIVE ME/US FREE ACCESS TO THE STRANGELIFE WORLDS. THEN, BROTHERS, SHALL WE/I FEED FULL! LINK NOW, AND OVERRIDE ITS FEEBLE EGO-SHELL, INCORPORATE IT INTO MY/OUR SELF-GESTALT, AND THEN ONWARD—ONWARD TO THE FEAST FOR WHICH WE/I HAVE SO LONG HUNGERED. MIND-STUFF IN ABUNDANCE TO SATIATE MY/OUR MOST EXTRAVAGANT FANTASIES OF REPLETION. LINK WELL, MY BROTHERS AND— BUT WHAT IS *THIS!*

The impact of Gool realization struck Granthan like the bursting of a great dam, and the overwhelming weight of the aroused alien intellect smashed him back, back. . . .

4

"How the hell did I get *here?*" Granthan wondered aloud. He was standing in the narrow accessway outside Power Section, supporting himself with a hand against the bulkhead. He remembered awakening, correcting the curiously distorted *vor* web, homing on the Brain Pit of the Great Race—and now he was here, aching from his massive wound, and from fatigue.

"Great appetite," he snorted aloud. "Ye gods, I came close to—whatever it was I came close to—but it kicked me out, thank God, and now I have a job to do. If that thing/those things should actually get loose on Terra—" He let the thought trail off.

"Now I have work to do," he told himself sternly. "I can hurt later. First, I have to get to Coign, before the poor bastard does something that can't be fixed. Brown." He spoke the name as if to reestablish the identity of the trivial speck of mind-stuff that was the powerman. The auxiliary access hatch to the Hot Box was before him. Might as well bull in as try to be cagey. On that thought he tried the 7-35G model hand-latch and the panel slid back on the mutter of voices amid a heavy stink of rotted flesh. Just inside the narrow compartment, the badly decomposed corpse of a man in fatigue uniform lay in the awkward slackness of death. It was a moment before Granthan realized, with shock, that it was Brown, and the advanced state of decomposition suggested how long he had

apparently been wandering, unconsciously, before
coming to himself outside Power Section. Granthan
snorted and stepped over the corpse, to confront a
frightened-looking Space'n Last Class who froze at
sight of him. Granthan gave the young fellow a reassuring smile and put a finger across his lips, miming
silence. The boy nodded and flattened himself against
the wall lockers as if to allow Granthan to pass.
Granthan shook his head and stepped back instead,
beckoning the lad to accompany him. He did so, hesitantly.

"Say," he blurted in a stage whisper, "ain't you
that civilian big-dome, Mr. Granthan? Sorry, sir, I
didn't mean, I mean, I only meant—"

"Sure," Granthan said softly as the worried-looking
youth came closer. "What happened to Brown?"
Granthan asked, nodding toward the heap of corrup-
tion on the deck.

"He came in and Chief shot him," the lad answered,
averting his eyes from the rotted corpse. Granthan put
a hand on his arm and said in a reassuring tone:

"We've got problems, Space'n—"

"Wiznieski, sir," the boy gulped. "They mostly call
me Whiz."

"Okay, Whiz, here's what we have to do," Granthan
said, sounding businesslike. "First, you need a
weapon." He handed over the piece he had taken from
Brown. Whiz took it gingerly.

"Gosh, sir, I never qualified on the Mark III," he
said apologetically.

"You probably won't need to fire it, Whiz,"
Granthan told the lad kindly. "Just point it if things
get that way." He heard a sound from around the

projecting corner of a storage locker and went flat against the bulkhead, motioning Whiz back. A burly arm and fist gripping a steel pry-bar flashed out and down through the space the lad had occupied a moment before. Granthan clamped a grip on the forearm and levered hard. The bar *clang!*ed on the deck. With a howl, a thickset Space'n First lunged out of concealment. He glared at Granthan wild-eyed.

"I ain't even *seen* you!" he yelled, sounding indignant. Whiz had his newly issued handgun in his fist, pointed at the newcomer.

"What's the idea, Jaw?" he demanded, sounding even more indignant than his assailant.

"'F you ain't in, you're on the other side," Jaw declared, then returned his attention to an attempt to climb the featureless bulkhead in an effort to relieve Granthan's pressure on his elbow. "You'll break it, you son of a swamper," Jaw yelped.

"That's a promise, Jaw," Granthan confirmed steadily. "Unless you quiet down and tell me what you think you're doing, trying to brain your shipmate."

"Skunk was listening in," Jaw blurted.

"On what?" Granthan demanded.

Jaw gave him a venomous look. "Nothing," he grunted and bared his teeth in a grimace as Granthan increased the pressure. "Leave me go and I'll tell you," the tormented man conceded.

Granthan released his arm. "Shoot him if he makes a move, Whiz," he ordered.

Whiz nodded. "He'd of busted my skull open," he said, wonderingly, and jabbed the pistol into Jaw's ribs.

"Step back a pace, Whiz," Granthan instructed the lad. "Keep clear of him."

"Just a few of the boys tryna figger what we gotta do," Jaw stated righteously.

"So you decided to ambush anybody who came along, is that the idea?" Granthan prompted.

"Can't trust nobody," Jaw grumbled, massaging his semisprained elbow. "Especially not you, you damned groundhog," he finished defiantly. Whiz jabbed the pistol at him again. Jaw whirled suddenly and grabbed for the gun, which uttered a muffled *squawk!* splattering Jaw's internal arrangements across smooth gray paint. Whiz jumped back as the bigger man collapsed.

Granthan drew and loaded his weapon; motioning Whiz to follow, he eased around the locker and confronted Warfield, gun in hand, three men behind him.

"Drop it, Chief," Granthan commanded. Whiz was close behind him. Instead of obeying, Warfield stepped back and yelled over his shoulder:

"Get clear, and scatter, boys! You know what to do!"

The men whirled and darted into concealment in the deep, shadowy recesses among the big coils and ducts which half filled the hold. Granthan let them go, restraining Whiz when he would have followed. The young fellow, gore-splattered, confronted Warfield. "I just shot Jaw," he growled. "And I'll shoot you, Chief, Mr. Granthan gives the word. You better follow orders." He glanced at Granthan for the kill order.

"Not yet, Whiz," Granthan said quietly. "Maybe never, if he smartens up."

"Sure," Whiz muttered, and stepped back a few

inches. "He'll smarten up, but if he tries anything . . ."

"Shoot if he even thinks about it," Granthan ordered. Warfield began to bluster:

"See to you later, you little punk," he snarled at Whiz, easing closer to Granthan, not threateningly, but as if for protection.

"Listen closely, Warfield," Granthan told the gray-faced powerman. "This ship is under attack. We're at war, like it or not. The Gool can meddle here, confuse people, give them incorrect ideas; but they can't actually do any material damage, it appears. All we have to do is maintain discipline and con this ship back closer to home where there's help available. We need to get a fix on these Gool. I have equipment back in my lab that can lock onto them and—maybe—take the offensive. So far all we've done is react the way they want us to. So, starting now, how about you deciding which side you want to be on."

"I'm a loyal Navy man, everybody knows that," Warfield blurted. "Only how'm I supposed to know which side you're working for, groundhog?"

"You're overworking that 'groundhog' tag," Granthan told the defensive NCO. "You'll have to use your head: what good would I get out of helping an alien entity destroy the ship I'm on, right along with precious you?"

Warfield was looking past Granthan's shoulder. "You kilt Jaw," he said. "Good powerman, Jaw. What'd you go and kill him for?"

"He was reluctant to abandon the idea that he could kill *us*," Granthan explained patiently. "Don't make the same mistake. Now, go round up those boys of yours and sit tight until you hear from Captain Coign."

"You got the captain, prolly tortured him until he agreed to do what you said," Warfield accused.

"Don't let your imagination work overtime," Granthan dismissed the charge. "Now, get back to your post of duty, and keep this power room hot, no matter what. Is that clear, Warfield?"

Warfield nodded. "Sure, that's clear, but I ain't working for no ghouls or whatever they are. I seen how they can make a good man go off his rails. Even done it to me," he concluded. "Had me thinking the whole place was afire. Funny, how they could do that."

"All they had to do was tickle your innate fear of fire a little," Granthan explained. "Your own imagination filled in the rest. Now beat it, and don't think I won't be back if you foul it up."

Warfield turned and ducked away into shadows, yelling for Joe.

"Shouldn't of let him go, sir," Whiz said, looking into the darkness where the senior powerman had disappeared.

"We can't hold the whole crew at gunpoint," Granthan reminded the boy patiently. "Now, Whiz, I have things to do. Can I leave you in charge here?"

"Well, I dunno, sir," Whiz temporized. "Must be six or eight of 'em: them three we seen, and the whole swing crew, too. I'll do my best." He hefted the big power gun.

"Just keep your eyes open, Whiz," Granthan counseled. "Don't let anybody sneak up on you, but don't shoot unless you have to—and if anything strange happens, sit tight. I'll be back in a few minutes." Without furthur preparation, he went back along the aisle and stepped out into the passage.

5

It was time, Granthan decided, to walk a tour of the ship; with Coign holding Command Deck and Power Section under control, the situation was at least temporarily stabilized.

He found the passageways mostly empty, the ship sounds around him normal. Most of the men seemed to be pulling duty as usual. In the galley, an immense superchief named Dolby assured him that meals would be forthcoming on time for all hands.

"The excitement seems to have quieted down, Mr. Granthan," he reported. "I had to coldcock a couple of fellows wanted to fight, but they'll be all right. No trouble for over an hour now." He folded his huge arms and smiled calmly. "Got plenty of stores, and as long as I've got power to my equipment, we'll eat. What's Cap'n Coign going do, Mr. Granthan? We heading home now?"

Granthan reassured the chef that he thought the vessel was bound for Terra and after eating a veal steak personally prepared by Chief Dolby, he continued on his rounds. Lighting and ship's communications were functioning normally, and the men he saw were all soberly doing their jobs. All was well aboard *Belshazzar*, it seemed. All he had to do now was relax and let the destiny of the Great Ones unfold, without any petty attempts to interfere with what must and would be. It was so right . . . and so easy . . . Granthan shook his head; he felt confused for a moment, as if he had been asleep on his feet. He was in a poorly lit passage behind the gymnasium. Suddenly, two smallish spacemen emerged abruptly from facing alcoves and stood in his path.

"What do you have in mind, fellows?" Granthan inquired genially.

"I seen what you did to Chief Warfield," one man said, and looked across at his partner for support.

"And just what did I do to your friend Chief Warfield?" Granthan asked.

"Nothing much," the gabby one replied. "Just blowed his head off."

"Whoever told you that brainless lie was just trying to get you in trouble, chum," Granthan said. "What's that name and number, now?" He made a production of taking out a pad and pen, looked inquiringly at the fellow.

"Bradshaw, isn't it?" he said. "Now the number, and then you can get the hell out of my way."

At that the two men lunged, arms-first, offering Granthan a choice of limbs to break. He selected one, clamped it in an elbow-cracking hold and said quietly to the other man, whom he had bounced against the bulkhead, "You don't mind waiting, I hope. I'll get to you in a moment. As for you, buster," he hissed in the gnarled ear of the man he was holding immobile, "if I let you keep this arm, will you take it away, and spend the next few hours in your quarters, meditating on your sins?"

"Sure, leave go," the man yelped, and Granthan released him. Both men retreated, muttering, and Granthan went on his way, alert for the next attack.

6

After two hours of quiet inspection he suddenly heard
a mutter of voices from around a turn in the passage.
He advanced cautiously and rounded the corner. A
few yards away a tight group of crewmen stood, silently eyeing him. Big Joe Bonzano was one of them;
he stepped forward.

"Oh, hiya, Mr. Granthan," he said dully, and
glanced aside from eye contact.

"What's happening, Joe?" Granthan asked casually. As if on signal, Bonzano charged, and Granthan
sidestepped, tripped the big fellow, who fell heavily.
Granthan then aimed his pistol at the CPO's head.

"Get up, Joe," he ordered curtly. Bonzano got to
his feet heavily. "Wasn't my fault," he muttered, looking at the floor. "They made me," he went on, more
briskly. "Said you were the one killed the cap'n."

"Coign's dead?" Granthan queried, feeling shock.
"That's bad, Bonzano. Who's conning the ship?"

"I was, until we got word you were in Power
Section, killed Warfield and the rest," Bonzano said
in a grumbling tone. "Said I was next. So what you
waiting for? You got yer Mark III, and I got nothing."
Granthan turned to look back at the men, who stood
uncertainly, awaiting the outcome of the parley, noticed a familiar face almost hidden in the rear rank.

"Come over here, Whiz," Granthan called, and
swiveled just in time to duck under Bonzano's hay-

maker and slam a straight left to the wild-eyed man's jaw. Bonzano folded, and as Granthan turned back to face the tight-clumped party of men, Whiz came up beside him.

"What's going on here?" Granthan demanded of the first-cruiser. "What are you doing in such unsavory company, Whiz? I thought you'd be one crewman I could count on not to join any wrecking crew."

"I didn't, sir," Whiz interrupted. "I'm their prisoner—sort of."

"Not anymore, Whiz," Granthan reassured the nervous lad. "What do they have in mind?" As Bonzano sat up suddenly, Granthan pushed him back with a foot in the face.

"Your turn will come, Joe," he told the now sobbing powerman.

"You blab, and I'll have yer innards for cargo-strapping, Whiz," Bonzano blustered, but subsided when Granthan kicked him gently in the ribs.

"Next one breaks bones, Joe," he said. "Now go on, Whiz." He returned his eyes to the young space'n.

"Told me how you shot the cap'n and all," Whiz offered defensively. "Said you were down here wiping out the duty crew." Whiz paused to glance worriedly at Bonzano's bloody face.

"Don't worry about him," Granthan encouraged. "What were they planning?"

"First, Chief said, we had to get *you*, Mr. Granthan," Whiz offered hesitantly, as if expecting to be shot where he stood. Granthan holstered the pistol.

"In spite of what Bonzano says, I'm not causing the trouble, Whiz," he said. "I don't know what you think happened, but I'm pretty sure the Gool have been tampering with you. We're under attack by an alien mind of great power, which has the ability to create illusions by playing with our minds. It seems to concentrate on the senior NCOs, experienced men, maybe because it can use their strong habits of discipline against them, but it must be following developments closely, and knew I'd left you in charge of Power Section."

"How are you feeling, Joe?" Granthan transferred his attention to Bonzano, who was now sitting up, dabbing at his bleeding nose with a grimy rag.

"Sorry about that nose," Granthan told him. "But you didn't leave me any room for finesse. Now, what do you say we stop clowning around and get this vessel into some kind of order?" Granthan reached out to pat Whiz's shoulder. "Take it easy, Space'n," he soothed as the slightly-built powerman shied at his touch. "I don't eat babies for breakfast," he added. "Now, would you like to be part of the solution, Whiz?" he queried seriously, holding the young fellow's eyes, until he wrenched his gaze away.

"What's wrong, Whiz?" Granthan asked in a kindly way. "Did Bonzano tell you I'd do a Svengali number on you, hypnotize you with my mesmeric eyes and make you climb up and sit on the ceiling?"

"A man doesn't know what to believe, sir," Whiz complained. "I want to do what's right, you know that, Mr. Granthan, sir. I always wanted to be a Navy man; I don't believe in mutiny. But with the captain dead and all—"

"Are you sure he's dead?" Granthan cut in. "Did you see the body?"

"Well, not exactly," Whiz replied. "But—Chief Bonzano said—"

"Sure," Granthan cut off the halting explanation.

"You'd better get back on the job, Whiz." Suddenly he felt a powerful impulse to start shooting: Bonzano, Whiz, anyone; after all, they were all against him. He fought against the intrusive urge. Granthan closed his eyes for concentration, and quickly ran through an orientation exercise, struggling to reground himself, shake free of Gool influence. From afar the ghostly voices clamored:

... HOLD TIGHT, BROTHERS! SEE HOW THE STRANGELIFE THRASHES IN OUR GRIP! THIS IS OUR ENEMY! FORGET THE LESSER ONES. HERE IS THE ONE WE MUST MASTER! LINK WELL, BROTHERS!

With an effort, Granthan pushed back against the relentless pressure. How easy it would be to relax and settle into the proffered new fabric of reality, rather than attempt longer to cling to the old, the invalid concept of human self-determination. It was not only a misguided effort, he realized with sudden clarity, it was a hopeless one. For an instant he perceived clearly the infinite subtlety and overwhelming rightness of the Gool reality-concept. Soon, he saw, all disharmony would vanish as everything fell into place in the Gool pattern, with lesser life-forms occupying their proper niches as supporters and sustainers of the Great Ones. Now, to simply relax and let the inevitable, the correct dominance of the Gool prevail. . . .

7

Granthan came to himself in the passage just by the lift to Command Deck. His Mark III was in his hand, and hot. Something had been happening. He rubbed a hand over his whiskery face, remembering the overwhelming (or perhaps only almost overwhelming) temptation to yield to the Gool mind-attack. It would have been (or had been) so blissfully easy. But how had he gotten here, two decks above where he had been? And where was Whiz? He called, heard only an echo. But before him the lift door stood open. He entered the cramped car; he was, he noticed, feeling fairly well, except for the huge fire in his shoulder and the numbness in his arm, which hung limp, bumping him as he moved. The door clashed shut and the car shot upward, braked to a halt almost at once, and the door slid back to reveal the chartroom, with Captain Coign working busily over the Fleet communications gear.

". . . care about that, Captain!" a harsh voice was saying, against the background crackling of the Belt. "Your orders are to extend your cruise by ten days standard, to oh-eight-hundred on six-nine; that's only a little over a week, after all, and it will give Deep Space Command time—"

"In a week, as matters stand, Admiral," Coign bellowed back, "the entire ship's complement will be dead or worse, and my command under the control

of this damned invisible whatsis this civilian wallah
Granthan calls the Gool! I've told you, sir, with re-
spect, you can't delay for a moment! A volley of six
Hannibal-class heads, spread forty degrees at contact
will do it; you have no choice, dammit, Admiral!
Better to lose a finger than the whole arm—hell, the
whole body politic! And I'm not striking a pose, dammit, I'd like to live to retire as much as any man—
but this thing is out of our experience and out of
control! Do it. Now!"

"Not quite yet, Captain," Granthan cut in, hearing
the blurriness of his own voice. He steadied himself
and stepped out to confront Coign, who spun to face
him, wild-eyed.

"That's an order, Captain," the braid-heavy voice
came from the talker. "Pick up the designated orbit
and report back in six hours."

"Six hours, my sitzfleisch, you damned pompous
old fool!" Coign yelled back, at the same time motioning Granthan to silence. He switched off his talker
and said in a quieter tone to Granthan:

"Got Starbird here: Damned old dotard thinks I've
got some kind of student Rag Day going on here. I
tried to tell him—"

"I know," Granthan cut him off. "I heard you.
Calling in a preemptive strike. The Captain Goes Down
with His Ship, eh? Forget it, Coign. We can lick this
thing."

"You don't know what you're meddling in,
Granthan," Coign snapped. "I can't risk—"

"Tsk," Granthan clucked. "I never thought I'd hear
an Annapolis man who's being 'groomed for high
command' propose to scuttle a capital ship of the Navy

with her fighting power intact, without a shot being fired."

"It's not that simple, dammit," Coign grumped. "If I take *Belshazzar* back to port while she's infected with—with whatever the hell she's infected with—"

"She's not infected, Captain," Granthan said soothingly. "We're under attack, but we're not helpless. We can resist, maybe even counterattack. Stop fighting me; let's work together and see what we can do."

Coign's eyes raked Granthan without sympathy. "You're not looking good, man," he complained. "I don't know what's holding you up. What the hell happened to you after I left you? I've had a rough time myself; had to shoot Ching—came at me with a cleaver. Got up here and found Starbird raving at me about not making the five-bells check-in on schedule. Damned old fool." Coign cut himself off abruptly, shot a glance at Granthan. "Tried to humor me," he grunted. "As if I were a schoolgirl swooning at the sight of a garter snake." He smacked a fist into his palm. "I tried to explain the situation, but he wouldn't listen, just shushed me and went on rattling about grave responsibilities, and serious reservations and the next round of promotions."

"As I recall, sir," Granthan commented without emphasis, "you yourself weren't especially sympathetic to the idea of a 'spook' attack when I first took the matter up with you. No one who hasn't experienced it can conceive—"

"Don't preach at me, Granthan!" Coign cut him off with a bellow. "Here, I'd better do something about that wound. Christ, I can see burned ribs down in there." He paused, looking a trifle pale, turned and went to the aid box, took out a kit, came back and began spraying sterifoam into the gaping pit in Granthan's living flesh. "Too bad I don't have a modern aid cabinet aboard," he muttered. "Bit of headquarters planning there: got 'em in the lifeboats, but none here. You sit down."

Granthan felt the potent medications in the foam begin to take effect: the pain receded to a remote ache, while his head seemed to clear. Suddenly it all seemed so simple.

"We've been making a mistake, Captain," he said. "Trying to oppose the Great One—or Ones." He paused, struggling to clarify the concept in his mind, and as he inspected the intangible thought-form, he recognized the telltale seam of discontinuity between his own and the invaders' ego-gestalt—

"Belay that, Captain," he managed, overriding the impulse to praise the Great Ones. "They're playing with my head, but I think I've got it under control." He put a hand to his face as if brushing away spiderwebs. Coign backed away.

"Granthan, maybe you'd better get back to your cabin," he suggested. "You're in bad shape, man. I'll help you."

"No, Captain, I'm as well here as elsewhere—and I think we should stay together. It will take both of us to beat this thing."

"No—my God—what can a man do?" Coign croaked, looking at Granthan with sick eyes. "When I can't even tell if my thoughts are my own? But I'm a naval officer, by God, and they'll not use *me* as a pawn." He drew his Mark III, put it to his throat. The detonations blew his jaw away. Granthan caught a glimpse of smashed and bleeding teeth gleaming white against red ruin as the captain collapsed before him.

"Swell," Granthan said aloud. "I guess that leaves it up to Mrs. Granthan's boy Pete." He went to the still-live talker and spoke into it:

"Fleet Headquarters, Granthan here, supercargo aboard *Belshazzar,* on station off Callisto. I have the honor to report the death in line of duty of Line-Captain Avram Coign, as well as Spacemen Brown and Ching, among others. We're in deep trouble here, but Captain Coign retained control of his command until the end. I now propose to do what I can. Over and out."

What he chiefly needed at the moment, Granthan reflected, was a good man to hold Command Deck while he himself got busy with the gear in his cabin. He thought of a tall log-room yeoman named Aloisius who had seemed an intelligent lad, and sufficiently gung ho to have earned the nickname "Admiral" among the deck crew. He went to the panel, and flipped keys marked GENERAL ADDRESS—HEAR THIS. Beside it was a crew roster: Granthan scanned it quickly.

"Space'n Aloisius Njaro will report to Command on the double," he said firmly. "All hands will co-operate to get him here ASAP."

Well, he thought, it might work. Good luck to the young fellow; he'd need it. Granthan turned to the spy-eye screen, keyed in the coordinates of Power Section. In the dimness of the big compartment, Whiz was visible, sitting on the floor; gun in hand.

"How goes it, Whiz?" Granthan asked. Whiz jumped in startlement, then looked straight at the spy-eye pickup.

"Oh, it's you, Mr. Granthan," he said unnecessarily. "Pretty quiet. I had to shoot Warfield," he added. "He jumped me. But the rest of his crew are at duty stations. I had 'em pitch Warfield and what was left of Brown in the waste converter, get a little use out of 'em."

"That's bad, Whiz. Warfield knew his Power Section. Send a man to the mess for food for all of you. And hang on. I should be able to relieve you soon."

Granthan then dialed the crew quarters, saw only a few men moving aimlessly through the cubicles. Admiral appeared, neatly turned out as usual. Dress blues in the middle of this cataclysm, Granthan pointed out to himself in wonder. Good man. Admiral passed from view, but Granthan worked dials, picked him up in the passage leading from Crew Country to the cargo area, where the nearest lift to upper decks was located. A couple of men were loitering there. Admiral ignored them and they did nothing as he passed, but fell in and followed to the lift. Aloisius used the call-key and stood waiting. One of his two shadows came up behind him. Suddenly, Aloisius spun about, and Granthan saw the glint of light on a steel blade in his hand. The honed edge whipped past the other man, a cargo-handler named Bliss, Granthan remembered.

"Missed!" Bliss spat, having jumped well back. Admiral looked at him thoughtfully, as the switchblade seemed to disappear into thin air. "Did you forget to do up your jacket, Georgie, or what?" he asked gently. Bliss looked down, fingering the open flaps of his deck-coat.

"All of the snaps is gone!" he stated. "Why, you—"

He made an abortive move, as if restraining himself with difficulty from attacking. "But you couldn'ta, not with one swipe o' that frog-sticker."

"Bye, Georgie," Admiral said and stepped back and into the waiting lift, just arrived.

The view switched to that provided by the eye in the car's ceiling. Admiral smoothed his unruffled hair, then stood quietly waiting, not quite standing at attention.

Granthan opened the narrow hatch giving ingress from the tiny anteroom as the lift door snapped back and Admiral stepped out. He saw Granthan.

"I believe it was you who called me up here, sir." he said.

"At ease, Space'n," Granthan said. "I like the way you handled Bliss and his friend," he went on. "Come on inside the sanctum and let's talk."

Admiral looked around curiously as he ducked under the overhead and squeezed himself flat against the bulkhead so as not to crowd the civilian bigshot. Then he saw the dead captain, and froze.

"Take it easy, Admiral," Granthan said, "or do you prefer Aloisius? Or Njaro?"

"That Jarro is some kind of Masai name, I heard," the spaceman replied. "I answer to Al, usually."

"Okay, Al," Granthan said. "Now, we have a situation on our hands here. Captain Coign died in line of duty. A brave man. I stepped in to do what I could. Now you can help. I think I have Power Section stabilized. Warfield's crew are back at their duty stations, and a fellow named Whiz is keeping an eye on things."

"Oh, Whiz, yeah, he's a pretty smart fellow, for a Polack," Admiral conceded. "'Polack' just means

'Pole' in Polish," he added seriously. "Not a bad name or anything."

"As long as we control Command Deck, and we have power," Granthan went on, "we have control of the situation. Now, I have to go out, get back to my quarters, and do what I can do to find out a little more about what we're up against."

"I want to help, Mr. Granthan," Njaro said, sounding nervous, "but I know just enough about the equipment up here in captain's country to know I don't know anything."

"All you have to do is sit tight until I get back," Granthan soothed. "Don't let anybody in under any circumstances. If you hear from Whiz, you can trust him. Nobody else. And even *he* doesn't get in here, okay?"

"If you say so, sir," Admiral agreed reluctantly. "Get back as soon as you can, if you please, Mr. Granthan. I don't mind telling you I'll be scared, up here all alone."

"I'd be scared up here if I had the Joint Chiefs of Staff to hold my hand," Granthan said. "But we can't let fear govern. We know what to do. Let's do it."

As Granthan turned to the general address talker to call Whiz, it suddenly became crystal clear to him that all he had to do now was relax, and the Great Ones would do the rest. So easy . . . and so right. . . .

DO IT, STRANGELIFE! LINK, BROTHERS. STRANGE-LIFE, LINK WITH US TO END THIS ANNOYANCE. KILL! KILL ALL WHO WOULD OPPOSE—

"Mr. Granthan!" Admiral's voice yelled from far away, but somehow close at hand, splitting the dreamy cocoon which had been almost sealed about Granthan.

He opened his eyes to see the ruined face of Captain Coign looming over him, blood dripping from the tip of the undamaged nose. A bubbly sound came from the shambles of the throat. Behind the dreadful apparition, Granthan saw Admiral's tear-streaked visage. Only inches away, Granthan looked at Coign's face—or half of it. The lower jaw was missing, and the upper teeth were exposed grotesquely against the bloody rags of the torn throat, from which blood pulsed in black-red waves.

"How'd he get up?" Admiral wailed. "He's dead! How can he stand up?" Admiral was openly weeping now. Granthan steadied him and said, "It's all right, Al, just another hallucination."

"What's the matter, Admiral?" a dull voice seemed to come from the torn mouth. "You and the civilian here gone off the rails together?"

"Oh, my God, Captain, you better sit down, sir," Admiral wailed. "You're hurt bad." He made a tentative move toward the bloody apparition, then flinched away. Coign's wide-open eyes were fixed on Granthan's face, though Granthan tried without success to make eye contact. He stepped forward and took the captain's arm, felt the solid flesh under the heavy blue polyon sleeve, heard the hoarse, bubbling breathing. A wave of dizziness washed over him; he felt the deck tilting underfoot.

"Mr. Granthan! Come on! You can't pass out now," the young fellow was shouting. He thrust past the ghastly Coign and seized Granthan's arm. "Get up, sir! You can't leave me here alone with that!" Admiral flinched from contact as the captain thrust him aside. Deliberately the thing that had been Captain Avram

G. (Goldie) Coign drew the heavy service pistol from the holster at its hip and took careful aim—not at Granthan, but behind him. Even as Granthan lunged to grapple the gun hand, the weapon fired a bolt of blue light with a sharp rasping sound. Behind him as he thrust the suddenly slack corpse away, Granthan heard the scrape and *thud!* of a body falling. He spun and looked down at Joe Bonzano's agonized face.

"Where—what—the big snake," Bonzano gasped before lapsing into silence. Granthan turned to see Admiral backing away, a horrified expression on his face.

"It—it," he stammered. Granthan called his name, sharply, and Admiral halted uncertainly.

"Dead officers don't walk around shooting people," Granthan told the terrified crewman. "Get hold of yourself, Al. The Gool have been playing with our heads, that's all."

"But," Admiral temporized, "but—*some*body shot Chief Bonzano!"

Granthan looked down at the heavy pistol in his hand. Had he . . . ? He didn't know. Coign lay slack at his feet, Bonzano beyond him.

"Al," Granthan said gently to the frightened man, "what did you see?"

"Saw Chief come in," Al said reluctantly. "Saw you shoot him down. Prolly had to, I guess, Mr. Granthan. I can testify he meant to attack you."

"Never mind, Al, just another trick," Granthan said soothingly. "I don't think Chief Bonzano is anywhere around here. He's probably in sick bay having his nose taped." He prodded the inert body with his foot.

"I don't know what to believe, Mr. Granthan,"

Admiral said hesitantly, "when a man can't believe his own eyes."

"That's what we're up against, Al," Granthan told the confused man. "We have to stay with basics: the ship is still intact and we can control her from here. We have to do what we can to pacify the crew, so they don't massacre each other. You can use the captain's spy-eye to check on the sick bay and mess. The men have to eat, and as long as there's somebody on duty to keep the food processors on line, no one will starve. Speaking of which, it's time to use the captain's autochef. What's your pleasure, Al? Beef Bourguignon, or hot dogs?"

"Neither one, Mr. Granthan," Al replied uneasily. "Not with *that* mess on the floor. Got no appetite."

"Hold the fort, Admiral," Granthan instructed the lad. "I have to get going now, and see what's happening. All this peace and quiet is getting on my nerves."

"I'll do my best, Mr. Granthan," Al said earnestly. "I just hope nobody tries to bust in here." He looked around, worriedly. "Mr. Granthan," he continued, "how come everything's so quiet?" He glanced at the big repeater board. "Looks like everything's cool," he commented. "Men must be pulling duty. Good luck, Mr. Granthan." Admiral offered his hand and Granthan shook it.

He went out into the anteroom, bypassed the lift and used the narrow companionway down to the crew-deck. The silence, except for the ever-present hum of the ship's routine functions, was complete. Granthan went to the barracks, looked in to see ranks of bunks, each with its sleeping occupant. Most of the off-duty crew, it appeared, were racking out after all the excitement.

Granthan prowled the long passages of the ship of the line, encountered only one man, Lewis, a gray-haired lieutenant commander, who was busy in Supply Section. He looked up curiously, as Granthan came in; his hand went to his holstered sidearm, then relaxed.

"Oh, it's you, Mr. Granthan," he said in a surprised tone. "I heard you were dead. Glad to see it's not true." Lewis nodded toward the inventory files he had been examining. "Just checking on reserves," he said, "just in case the crazy business resumes."

"Has it ever stopped, Commander?" Granthan asked the round-shouldered officer. "I've been too busy to notice."

"For the past week, things have been pretty stable. Except, of course, for the disappearances of Captain Coign, and a few others. We formed an officer's committee to run things until the captain turns up."

"He's dead, Commander," Granthan told the man gently. "You and your committee had better stay in charge a little longer. Are you planning to con her back to Terran orbit pretty soon?"

"That depends," Lewis said, wagging his head. "Commander Dwight says we've been ordered to sheer off and pick up a solar orbit. I don't know what that could accomplish."

"It would keep us at arm's length while High Command decides what to do with us," Granthan suggested.

"That's true," Lewis agreed, "but what do you mean, 'do with us'? I assume we'll receive a hero's welcome for surviving the enemy attack with so few casualties."

"Don't count on it," Granthan advised. "Captain Coign called for an interdictory strike."

Lewis's face went stiff and clay-colored. "How long?" he asked.

"I don't know if Deep Space Command plans to honor his request," Granthan explained. "He was pretty upset when he was talking with the admiral."

"I'll check with Communications Section," Lewis offered. "If you'll excuse me," he added diffidently, and went into the cubbyhole log room to busy himself at the shipboard talker. When he reemerged, he look like a man who had been struck in the solar plexus by a straight left jab.

"Ted says a flight of twenty Ajax-class—closing at full speed. He suggested a council meeting, five minutes, on Command Deck. Would you care to attend?"

"What can we do?" Granthan asked. "Does Shazzy have the capability to evade or outrun the missiles?"

"No way," Lewis said gloomily. "Best we can do is maybe intercept 'em with a salvo of our own. That's up to Bucky, the gunnery officer."

8

Lieutenant Commander Buckingham, lean, gray-haired, and impeccably uniformed as always, spoke in the diffident tones of an undertaker presenting his bill.

"There's nothing else I can suggest, gentlemen," he commented. "We still have time to abandon ship before entering the Zone yellow conic, and with a little luck, the Jacks will ignore the lifeboats."

As the ranking officer, Commander Endor, red-faced and overweight in grade, rose to speak, the lights dimmed; the deck tilted, pressing upward with the relentless inertia of an avalanche.

"Automatics are taking evasive action," Brent, the troop commander, yelled. "Your numbers must be off, Bucky! They're here!"

White light flashed, blindingly. Through the dusty glare, Granthan saw yelling men sliding, falling, grabbing for handholds on furnishings which were themselves adrift, starting a pileup at the bulkhead, while *thump!*s and sounds of breakage drowned the attempts at command. He found himself against the ventilator grille, which collapsed, precipitating him into the echoic sheet-metal duct, in free-fall, to slam at last against a solid obstruction. Half dazed, he managed to marshal his thoughts and to focus his awareness on the intrusive touch which dimmed the pain of a badly fractured femur, brushed aside sensation of the fire which was impalpably caressing him, the screaming agony as skin blackened and burned, flesh roasted, bubbled, and burst. As one swathed in anesthetic foam, he groped, half aware that it was the intruding Gool presence that was forcing him to crawl, skirting the exploded heat exchanger, find the escape route, plunge down the shaft to the lifeboat deck. The ship was tumbling now—and it was not illusion—of that he was quite sure. And if the Gool were controlling him, fine—as long as they were steering him away from the relentless flames. He caught a glimpse of his charred hand, scrabbling for a grip on the lifeboat's port lock; then a blast, a *boom!* that shattered his consciousness into fragments finer than dust motes, which drifted for an unmeasured time before coalescing once again into the knowledge that somehow he had escaped, was aboard a lifeboat, though somehow still adrift in a torrent of fire. The insidious touch of the Gool was gone. He was alive, and free. Then all thought ceased.

CHAPTER
THREE

1

BELSHAZZAR SURVIVOR FOUND?

Sitting at his eight-foot rosewood desk at HQ, Deep Space Command, Admiral-General Margrave scanned the item from the Singapore *Times-Standard,* included in the morning's CMRP folder.

"Hmmph," he muttered as he tossed the clipping aside. "Look into this, Freddy," he commanded the middle-aged commander serving as his press aide. "Some damned nut, no doubt," he went on. "According to the clip, he was found combing the beach on some island in the Dalhousie Group. But we'll have to check it out." He sighed heavily, shifted his foot from the corner of the desk to lean back, feet on the floor, unconsciously and instinctively assuming a position of readiness for combat.

"The first time in history a battleship of the Space Arm has been lost in space," he said dully, to no one.

"Even if I did order it blasted myself. And nothing to show for it but some garbled transmissions from Goldie Coign. Used to be a good man."

"There *was* the matter of the disappearing lifeboat," the aide suggested cautiously. "The one Luna Base failed to recover."

"Art Kayle's alibi," Margrave snorted. "But follow this up, Freddy, and unless the fellow's a raving psychotic, get him in here. Fast. If he's genuine, I have to pick his brain clean."

"The Admiral recalls the curious business at Denver last week," Freddy offered hesitantly. "You don't suppose, sir, there's any possible connection—"

"I never suppose," Margrave grumped. "That damned civilian, Grantland or whatever, was supposed to have penetrated the vault, only there was nobody there, as I recall. I see no connection other than that Security Command is in serious need of a shaking-up. Freddy, get me the file on that fiasco."

"Sir," Freddy said nervously, "the next item I had for you, sir, is a statement compiled from six taped interviews with this beachcomber fellow. For your eyes only, of course, sir."

"Brief it, and I'll look it over after lunch," Margrave commanded. "Here, I'll initial it." He scribbled on the cover of the EO document: "released to Cmdr. Phipps for résumé. M." Then he turned his eyes to the mimeographed sheets.

2

A VOLUNTARY STATEMENT BY PETER GRANTHAN, PH.D.

In the dream I was swimming in a river of white fire. The dream went on and on; and then I was awake— and the fire was still there, burning fiercely at me.

I moved to get away from the flames, and the real pain hit me. I tried to go back to sleep and the relative comfort of the river of fire, but it was no go. For better or worse, I was alive and conscious.

I opened my eyes and took a look around. I was on the floor next to an unpadded acceleration couch— the kind the Terrestrial Space Arm installs in seldom-used lifeboats. There were three more couches, but no one in them. I tried to sit up. It wasn't easy but, by applying a lot more willpower than should be required of a sick man, I made it. I took a look at my left arm. Bad. The hand was only medium rare, but the forearm was black, with deep red showing at the bottom of the cracks where the crisped upper layers had burst. My right shoulder was the next item to check: all I could see was a dirty mass of sterifoam.

The first-aid cabinet was across the compartment from me. I tried my right leg, felt broken bone ends grate with a sensation that transcended pain. I heaved with the other leg, scrabbled with the charred arm. The crawl to the cabinet dwarfed Hillary's trek up Everest, but I reached it after a couple of years, and found the microswitch on the floor that activated the thing, and then I was fading out again. . . .

3

I came out of it this time clearheaded but weak. My right leg was numb, but reasonably comfortable, clamped tight in a walking brace. I put up a hand and felt a shaved skull, with sutures. It must have been a fracture. For a moment I had a ghostly memory of falling down an elevator shaft. The right arm—well, it was still there, wrapped to the shoulder and held out stiffly by a power truss that would keep the scar tissue from pulling up and crippling me. The steady pressure as the truss contracted wasn't anything to do a sense-tap on for replaying at leisure moments, but at least the cabinet hadn't amputated. I wasn't complaining. The right forearm had been foamed and wrapped.

As far as I knew, I was the first recorded survivor of contact with the Gool—if I survived.

I was still a long way from home, and I hadn't yet checked on the condition of the lifeboat. I glanced toward the entry port. It was dogged shut. I could see black marks where my burned hand had touched it.

I fumbled my way into a couch and tried to think. In my condition—with a broken leg and third-degree burns, plus a fractured skull—I shouldn't have been able to fall out of bed, much less make the trip from *Belshazzar*'s Command Deck to the boat; and how had I managed to dog that port shut? In an emergency a man was capable of great exertions. But running on a broken femur, handling heavy levers with charred fingers and thinking with a cracked head were overdoing it. Still, I was here—and it was time to get a call through to TSA headquarters.

I flipped the switch and gave the emergency call letters Colonel Ausar Kayle of Aerospace Intelligence had assigned to me a few weeks before. It was almost five minutes before the "acknowledge" came through from the Ganymede relay station, another ten minutes before Kayle's face swam into view. Even through the blur of the screen I could see the haggard look.

"Granthan!" he burst out. "Where is Captain Coign? What happened out there?" I turned him down to a mutter.

"Hold on," I said. "I'll tell you. Recorders going?" I didn't wait for an answer—not with a fifteen-minute transmission lag. I plowed on:

"Belshazzar was sabotaged by her own crew—against their will. Then we were hit. I got out. I lost a little skin, but the aid cabinet has the case in hand. Tell the med people the drinks are on me."

I finished talking and flopped back, waiting for Kayle's reply. On the screen, his flickering image gazed back impatiently, looking as hostile as a swingshift ward nurse. It would be half an hour before I would get his reaction to my report. I dozed off—and awoke with a start. Kayle was talking.

"—your report. I won't mince words. They're wondering at your role in the disaster. How does it happen that you alone survived?"

"How the hell do I know?" I yelled—or croaked.

But Kayle's voice was droning on:

"Y . . . your psychodynamics people have been telling me that Gool may have some kind of long-range telehypnotic ability that might make it possible for them to subvert a loyal man without his knowledge. You've told me yourself that you blacked out during the attack—and came to on the lifeboat, with no recollection of how you got there.

"This is war, Granthan. War against a vicious enemy who strikes without warning and without mercy. You were sent out to investigate the possibility of— what's that term you used—hypercortical invasion. You know better than most the risk I'd be running if you were allowed to pass the patrol line.

"I'm sorry, Granthan. I can't let you land on Terra. I can't accept the risk."

"What do I do now?" I stormed. "Go into orbit and eat pills and hope you think of something? I need a whole pest-house full of doctors!"

Presently Kayle replied. "Yes," he said. "You'll have to enter a parking orbit. Perhaps there will be developments soon which will make it possible to . . . ah . . . restudy the situation." He didn't meet my eye. I knew what he was thinking. He'd spare me the mental anguish of knowing what was coming. I couldn't really blame him; he was doing what he thought was the right thing. And I'd have to go along and pretend—right up until the warheads struck— that I didn't know I'd been condemned to death.

4

I tried to gather my wits and think my way through the situation. I was alone and injured, aboard a lifeboat that would be the focus of a converging flight of missiles as soon as I approached within battery range of Terra. I had gotten clear of the Gool, but I wouldn't survive my next meeting with my own kind. They couldn't take the chance I was acting under Gool orders.

I wasn't, of course. I was still the same Peter Granthan, psychodynamicist, who had started out with Coign's command nine weeks earlier. The thoughts I was having weren't brilliant, but they were mine, all mine. . . .

But how could I be sure of that?

Maybe there was something in Kayle's suspicion.

If the Gool were as skillful as we thought, they would have left no overt indications of their tampering—not at a conscious level.

But this was where psychodynamics training came in. I had been reacting like any scared casualty, aching to get home and lick his wounds. But I wasn't just any casualty. I had been trained in the subtleties of the mind—and I had been prepared for just such an attack.

Now was the time to make use of that training. It had given me at least one useful resource. I could unlock the memories of my subconscious—and see what had happened.

I lay back, cleared my mind of extraneous thoughts, and concentrated on the trigger word that would key an autohypnotic sequence. . . .

Sense impressions faded. I was alone in the nebulous emptiness of a first-level trance. I keyed a second word, slipped below the misty surface into a dreamworld of vague phantasmagoric figures milling in their limbo of subconceptualization. I penetrated deeper, broke through into the vividly hallucinatory third level, where images of mirror-bright immediacy clamored for attention. And deeper . . .

5

The immense orderly confusion of the basic memory level lay before me. Abstracted from it, aloof and observant, the monitoring Personality Fraction scanned the pattern, searching the polydimensional continuum for evidence of an alien intrusion.

And found it.

As the eye instantaneously detects a flicker of motion amid an infinity of static detail, so my inner eye perceived the subtle traces of the probing Gool mind, like a whispered touch deftly rearranging my buried motivations.

I focused selectively, tuned to the recorded gestalt.

IT IS A CONTACT, EFFULGENT ONE!

SOFTLY, NOW! NURTURE THE SPARK WELL. IT BUT TREMBLES AT THE THRESHOLD . . .

THE STRANGELIFE IS ELUSIVE, MASTER! IT WRIG-

GLES LIKE A GORM-WORM IN THE EATING TROUGH!

A part of my mind watched as the memory un-reeled. I listened to the voices—yet not voices, merely the shapes of concepts, indescribably intricate. I saw how the decoy pseudopersonality which I had con-cretized for the purpose in a hundred training sessions had fought against the intruding stimulus—then yielded under the relentless thrust of the alien probe. I watched as the Gool operator took over the motor centers, caused me to crawl through the choking smoke of the devasted mechanical equipment compartment toward the shaft to the lifeboat dock. Fire from the wrecked heat exchanger leaped up, blocking the way. I went on, felt ghostly flames whipping at me—and then the hatch was open and I pulled myself through, forcing the broken leg. I remembered my blackened hand fumbling at the locking wheel; then the blast as the lifeboat leaped clear of the disintegrating dread-nought—and the world-ending impact as I fell.

At a level far below the conscious, the embattled pseudopersonality lashed out again—fighting the in-vader, and eliciting instant response:

ALMOST IT ELUDED ME THEN, EFFULGENT LORD. LINK WITH THIS LOWLY ONE!

IMPOSSIBLE! DO YOU FORGET ALL MY TEACHINGS? CLING, THOUGH YOU EXPEND THE LAST FILAMENT OF YOUR LIFE-FOCUS!

Free from all distraction, at a level where compre-hension and retention are instantaneous and total, my monitoring basic Personality Fraction followed the skillful Gool mind as it engraved its command deep in my subconscious. Then the touch withdrew, erasing the scars of its passage, to leave me unaware of its tampering—at a conscious level.

Watching the Gool mind, I learned.

The insinuating probe—a concept regarding which psychodynamicists had theorized—was no more than a pattern in emptiness. . . .

But a pattern which I could duplicate, now that I had seen what had been done to me.

Hesitantly, I felt for the immaterial fabric of the continuum, warping and manipulating it, copying the Gool probe. Like planes of paper-thin crystal, the polyfinite aspects of reality shifted into focus, aligning themselves.

Abruptly, a channel lay open. As easily as I would stretch out my hand to pluck a moth from a nightflower, I reached across the unimaginable void—and sensed a pit blacker than the bottom floor of hell, and a glistening dark shape.

There was a soundless shriek. EFFULGENCE! IT REACHED OUT—TOUCHED ME!

6

Using the technique I had grasped from the Gool itself, I struck, stifling the outcry, invaded the fetid blackness and grappled the obscene gelatinous immensity of the Gool spy as it spasmed in a frenzy of xenophobia— a ton of liver writhing at the bottom of a dark well, exuding hate.

I clamped down control. The Gool mind folded in on itself, gibbering. Not pausing to rest, I followed up, probed along my channel of contact, tracing patterns, scanning the flaccid Gool mind. . . .

I saw a world of yellow seas lapping at endless shores of mud. There was a fuming pit, where liquid sulfur bubbled up from some inner source, filling an immense natural basin. The Gool clustered at its rim, feeding, each monstrous shape heaving against its neighbors for a more favorable position.

I probed farther, saw the great cables of living nervous tissue that linked each eating organ with the brain-mass far underground. I traced the passages through which tendrils ran out to immense caverns where smaller creatures labored over strange devices. These, my host's memory told me, were the young of the Gool. Here they built the fleets that would transport the spawn to the new worlds the Prime Overlord had discovered, worlds where food was free for the taking. Not sulphur alone, but potassium, calcium, iron and all the metals—riches beyond belief in endless profusion. No longer would the Gool tribe cluster—those who remained of a once-great race—at a single feeding trough. They would spread out across a galaxy—and beyond.

But not if I could help it. But could I help it?

The Gool had evolved a plan—but they'd had a stroke of bad luck.

In the past, they had managed to control a man here and there, among the fleets, far from home, but only at a superficial level. Enough, perhaps, to wreck a ship, but not the complete control needed to send a man back to Terra under Gool compulsion, to carry out complex sabotage.

They had trailed me, alone, a sole survivor, free

from the clutter of the other Strangelife mind-fields. It had been their misfortune to pick a psychodynamicist. Instead of gaining a patient slave, they had opened the fortress door to an unseen spy. Now that I was there, I would see what I could steal.

A timeless time passed. I wandered among patterns of white light and white sound, plumbed the deepest recesses of hidden Gool thoughts, fared along strange ways examining the shapes and colors of the concepts of an alien mind.

I paused at last, scanning a multiordinal structure of pattern within pattern; the diagramed circuits of a strange machine.

I followed through its logic sequence; and, like a bomb-burst, its meaning exploded in my mind.

From the vile nest deep under the dark surface of the Gool world in its lonely eccentric orbit, I had plucked the ultimate secret of their kind:

Matter across space.

7

"You've got to listen to me, Kayle," I shouted into the talker, "I know you think I'm a Gool robot. But what I have is too big to let you blow it up without a fight. Matter transmission! You know what that can mean to us. The concept is too complex to try to describe in words. You'll have to take my word for it. I can build it, though, using standard components, plus an infinite-area antenna and a Möbius-wound coil—and a few other things. . . ."

I harangued Kayle for a while, and then sweated out his answer. I was getting close now. If he couldn't see the beauty of my proposal, my screens would start to register the radiation of warheads any time now.

Kayle came back—and his elaborate answer boiled down to "no."

I tried to reason with him. I reminded him how I had readied myself for the trip with simulation sessions on the encephaloscope, setting up the cross-networks of conditioned responses, the shunt circuits to the decoy pseudopersonality, leaving my volitional ego free. I talked about subliminal hypnotics and the resilience quotient of the ego-complex.

I might have saved my breath.

"I don't understand that psychodynamics jargon, Granthan," he snapped. "It smacks of mysticism. But I understand what the Gool have done to you well enough. I'm sorry."

I leaned back and chewed the inside of my lip and thought unkind thoughts about Colonel Ausar Kayle. Then I settled down to solve the problem at hand.

I keyed the chart file, flashed pages from the standard index on the reference screen, checking radar coverages, beacon ranges, monitor stations, controller fields. It looked as though a radar-negative boat the size of mine might possibly get through the defensive net with a daring pilot, and as a condemned spy, I could afford to be daring.

And I had a few ideas.

8

The shrilling of the proximity alarm blasted through the silence. For a wild moment I thought Kayle had beaten me to the punch; then I realized it was the routine DEW line patrol contact.

"Z four-oh-two, I am reading your IFF," the talker said tonelessly. "Decelerate at one point eight gee preparatory to picking up approach orbit..."

The screen went on droning out instructions. I fed them into the autopilot, at the same time running over my approach plan. The patrol boat off my port bow was moving in closer. I licked dry lips. It was time to try.

I closed my eyes, reached—as the Gool mind had reached out to me—and felt the touch of a signals officer's mind, 40,000 miles distant, aboard the patrol vessel. There was a brief flurry of struggle; then I dictated my instructions. The signals officer punched keys, spoke into his talker:

"As you were, Z four-oh-two. Continue on present course. At oh-nineteen seconds, pick up Planetary for reentry and letdown."

Easily, I blanked out the man's recollection of what had happened, caught his belated puzzlement as I broke contact. But I was clear of the DEW line now, rapidly approaching atmosphere. Then the long-range talker boomed out:

"Z four-oh-two," the speaker crackled. "This is Planetary Control. I am picking you up on channel forty-three, for reentry and letdown."

There was a long pause. Then: "Z four-oh-two, countermand DEW line clearance! Repeat, clearance countermanded! Emergency course change to standard hyperbolic code ninety-eight. Do not attempt reentry. Repeat: do not attempt reentry!"

It hadn't taken Kayle long to see that I'd gotten past the outer line of defense. A few more minutes' grace would have helped. I'd play it dumb, and hope for a little luck.

"Planetary, Z four-oh-two here. Say, I'm afraid I missed part of that, fellows. I'm a little banged up— I guess I switched frequencies on you. What was that after 'pick up channel forty-three' . . . ?"

"Four-oh-two, sheer off there! You're not cleared for reentry!"

"Hey, you birds are mixed up," I protested. "I'm cleared all the way. I checked in with DEW—"

It was time to disappear. I blanked off all transmission, hit the controls, following my evasive pattern. And again I reached out, farther this time. . . .

A radar man at a site in the Pacific, 15,000 miles away, rose from his chair, crossed the darkened room and threw switches. The radar screens blanked off. . . .

For an hour I rode the long orbit down, while the autopilot warded off attack after attack. Then I was clear, skimming the surface of the ocean a few miles southeast of Key West. The boat hit hard. I felt the floor rise up, over, buffeting me against the restraining harness.

I hauled at the release lever, felt a long moment of giddy disorientation as the emergency module separated from the sinking lifeboat deep under the surface. Then my escape capsule was bobbing on the water.

I would have to risk calling Kayle now—but by voluntarily giving my position away, I might convince him I was still on our side—and I was badly in need of a pickup. I flipped the sending key.

"This is Z four-oh-two," I said. "I have an urgent report for Colonel Kayle of Aerospace Intelligence."

Kayle's face appeared on the miniature screen, looking even more haggard. "Don't fight it, Granthan," he croaked. "You penetrated the planetary defenses— God knows how. I—"

"Later," I snapped. "How about calling off your dogs now? And send somebody out here to pick me up, before I add seasickness to my other complaints."

"We have you pinpointed," Kayle cut in. "It's no use fighting it, Granthan."

9

I yelled: "You've got to listen, Kayle! I suppose you've got missiles on the way already. Call them back! I have information that can win the war—"

"I'm sorry, Granthan," Kayle said. "It's too late— even if I could take the chance you were right."

A different face appeared on the screen.

"Mr. Granthan, I am General Titus. On behalf of your country, and in the name of the President—who has been apprised of this tragic situation—it is my privilege to inform you that you will be awarded the

Congressional Medal of Honor—posthumously—for your heroic effort. Although you failed, and have in fact been forced, against your will, to carry out the schemes of the inhuman enemy, this in no way detracts from your gallant attempt. Mr. Granthan, I salute you."

The general's arm went up in a rigid gesture.

"Stow that, you pompous idiot!" I barked. "I'm no spy!"

Kayle was back, blanking out the startled face of the general.

"Good-bye, Granthan. Try to understand..."

I flipped the switch, sat gripping the couch, my stomach rising with each heave of the floating capsule. I had perhaps five minutes. The missiles would be from Canaveral.

I closed my eyes, forced myself to relax, reached out, straining...

I sensed the distant shore, the hot buzz of human minds at work in the cities. I followed the coastline, found the missile base, flicked through the cluster of minds.

—*missile on course; do right, baby. That's it, right in the slot.*

I fingered my way through the man's mind and found the control centers. He turned stiffly from the plotting board, tottered to a panel to slam his hand against the destruct button.

Men fell on him, dragged him back. "—fool, why did you blow it?"

I dropped the contact, found another, who leaped to the panel, detonated the remainder of the flight of six missiles. Then I withdrew. I would have a few minutes' stay of execution now.

I was ten miles from shore. The capsule had its own power plant. I started it up, switched on the external viewer. I saw dark sea, the glint of starlight on the choppy surface, in the distance a glow on the horizon that would be Key West. I plugged the course into the pilot, then leaned back and felt outward with my mind for the next attacker.

10

It was dark in the trainyard. I moved along under the rail in a stumbling walk. Just a few more minutes and you can lie down . . . rest . . .

The shadowed bulk of a monorail cargo car loomed up, its open door a blacker square. I leaned against the sill, breathing hard, then reached inside for a grip with my good hand.

Gravel scrunched nearby. The beam of a flashlight lanced out, slipped along the weathered car, caught me. There was a startled exclamation. I ducked back, closed my eyes, felt out for his mind. There was a confused murmur of thought, a random intrusion of impressions from the city all around. It was hard, too hard. I had to sleep—

I heard the snick of a revolver being cocked, and dropped flat as a gout of flame stabbed toward me, the imperative *bam!* echoing between the cars. I caught the clear thought:

God-awful looking, shaved head, arm stuck out; him, all right—

I reached out to his mind and struck at random. The light fell, went out, and I heard the unconscious body slam to the ground like a pole-axed steer.

It was easy—if I could only stay awake.

I gritted my teeth, pulled myself into the car, crawled to a dark corner behind a crate and slumped down. I tried to evoke a Personality Fraction to set as a guard, a part of my mind to stay awake and warn me of danger. It was too much trouble. I relaxed and let it all slide down into darkness.

11

The car swayed, *tic-tic-tic*. I opened my eyes, saw yellow sunlight in a bar across the litter on the floor. The power truss cracked, pulling at my arm. My broken leg was throbbing its indignation at the treatment it had received—walking brace and all—and the burned arm was yelling aloud for more of that nice dope that had been keeping it from realizing how bad it was. All things considered, I felt like a badly embalmed mummy—except that I was hungry. I had been a fool not to fill my pockets when I left the escape capsule in the shallows off Key West, but things had been happening too fast.

I had barely made it to the fishing boat, whose owner I had coerced into rendezvousing with me before shells started dropping around us. If the gunners on the cruiser ten miles away had had any luck, they would have finished me—and the hapless fisherman—right then. We rode out a couple of near misses, before I put the cruiser's gunnery crew off the air.

At a fishing camp on the beach, I found a car—with driver. He dropped me at the railyard, and drove off under the impression he was in town for groceries. He'd never believe he'd seen me.

Now I'd had my sleep. I had to start getting ready for the next act of the farce.

I pressed the release on the power truss, gingerly unclamped it, then rigged a sling from a strip of shirt-tail. I tied the arm to my side as inconspicuously as possible. I didn't disturb the bandages.

I needed new clothes—or at least different ones—and something to cover my shaved skull. I couldn't stay hidden forever. The yard cop had recognized me at a glance.

I lay back, waiting for the train to slow for a town. I wasn't unduly worried—at the moment. The watch-man probably hadn't convinced anyone he'd actually seen me. Maybe he hadn't been too sure himself.

The *tic-tic* slowed and the train shuddered to a stop. I crept to the door, peered through the crack. There were sunny fields, a few low buildings in the distance, the corner of a platform. I closed my eyes and let my awareness stretch out, made contact:

—*lousy job. What's the use? Little witch in the lunch room . . . up in the hills, squirrel hunting, bottle of whiskey . . .*

I settled into control gently, trying not to alarm the man. I saw through his eyes the dusty boxcar, the rust on the rail, the listless weeds growing among cinders around the pylon, and the weathered PVC of the plat-form. I turned him, and saw the dingy glass of the telegraph window, a sagging screen door with a chipped enamel cola sign.

I walked the man to the door, and through it. Behind a linoleum-topped counter, a coarse-skinned teenage girl with heavy breasts and wet patches under her arms looked up without interest as the door banged.

My host went on to the counter, gestured toward the waxed-paper-wrapped sandwiches under a glass cover. "I'll take 'em all. And candy bars, and cigarettes. And give me a big glass of water."

"Better git out there and look after yer train," the girl said carelessly. "When'd you git so all-fired hungry all of a sudden?"

"Put it in a bag. Quick."

"Look who's getting bossy—"

My host rounded the counter, picked up a used paper bag, began stuffing food in it. The girl stared at him, then pushed him back. "You git back around that counter! I'll call Fred!"

We retreated.

She filled the bag, took a pencil from behind her ear.

"That'll be six eighty-five. Cash."

My host took two dog-eared bills from his shirt pocket, dropped them on the counter and waited while the girl filled a glass. He picked it up and started out.

"Hey! Where you goin' with my glass?"

The trainman crossed the platform, headed for the boxcar above the platform. He climbed up, slid the loose door back a few inches against the slack latch, put the bag inside, placed the glass of water beside it through the opening. He turned. The girl watched from the platform. A rattle passed down the line and the train started up with a lurch. The man walked back toward the girl. I heard him say: "Friend o' mine in there—just passin' through." He was on his own now.

I was discovering that it wasn't necessary to hold tight control over every move of a subject. Once given the impulse to act, he would rationalize his behavior, fill in the details—and never know that the original idea hadn't been his own.

I drank the water first, ate a sandwich, then lit a cigarette and lay back. So far so good. The crates in the car were marked U.S. NAVAL AEROSPACE STATION, BAYOU LE COCHON. With any luck I'd reach New Orleans in another twelve hours. The next step of my plan included a raid on the Delta National Labs; but that was tomorrow. That could wait.

12

It was a little before dawn when I crawled out of the car and dropped the six feet to the gravel, at a siding in the swampy country a few miles out of New Orleans. I wasn't feeling good, but I had a stake in staying on my feet. I still had a few miles in me. I had my supplies—a few candy bars and some cigarettes—stuffed in the pockets of the tattered issue coverall. Otherwise, I was unencumbered. Unless you wanted to count the walking brace on my right leg and the sling binding my arm, and the greasy railroader's cap.

I picked my way across mushy ground to a potholed

blacktop road, started limping toward a truck's lights visible half a mile away. It was already hot. The swamp air was like warmed-over subway fumes. Through the drugs, I could feel my pulse throbbing in my various wounds. I reached out and touched the driver's mind; he was thinking about shrimps, a fishhook wound on his left thumb and a girl with black hair. "Want a lift?" he called when I came up to the pickup.

I thanked him and got in. He gave me a glance and I pinched off his budding twinge of curiosity. It was almost an effort now *not* to follow his thoughts. It was as though my mind, having learned the trick of communicating with others, instinctively reached out toward them.

An hour later he dropped me on a street corner in a shabby marketing district of the city and drove off. I hoped he made out all right with the dark-haired girl. I spotted a used-clothing store and headed for it.

Twenty minutes later I was back on the sidewalk, dressed in a pinkish-gray suit that had been cut a long time ago by a Latin tailor—maybe to settle a grudge. The shirt that went with it was an unsuccessful violet. The black string tie lent a dubious air of distinction. I'd swapped the railroader's cap for a tarnished beret. The man who had supplied the outfit was still asleep. I figured I'd done him a favor by taking it. I couldn't hope to pass for a fisherman—I wasn't the type. Maybe I'd get by as a coffeehouse derelict.

I walked past fly-covered fish stalls, racks of faded garments, grimy vegetables in bins, past paint-flaked wrought iron, and fetched up at a cab stand. I picked a fat driver with a wart.

"How much to the Delta National Laboratories?"

He rolled an eye toward me, shifted his toothpick.

"What ya wanna go out there for? Nothing out there."

"I'm a tourist," I said. "They told me before I left home not to miss it."

He grunted, reached back and opened the door. I got in. He flipped his flag down, started up with a clash of gears and pulled out without looking.

"How far is it?" I asked him.

"It ain't far. Mile, mile and a quarter."

"Pretty big place, I guess."

He didn't answer.

We went through a warehousing district, swung left along the waterfront, bumped over potholed blacktop, and pulled up at a nine-foot cyclone fence with a locked gate.

"A buck ten," my driver said.

I looked out at the fence, a barren field, a distant group of low buildings. "What's this?"

"This is the place you ast for. That'll be a buck ten, mister."

I touched his mind, planted a couple of false impressions and withdrew. He blinked, then started up, drove around the field, pulled up at an open gate with a blue-uniformed guard. He looked back at me.

"You want I should drive in, sir?"

"I'll get out here."

He jumped out, opened my door, helped me out with a hand under my good elbow. "I'll get your change, sir," he said, reaching for his hip.

"Keep it."

"Thank *you*." He hesitated. "Maybe I oughta stick around. You know."

"I'll be all right."

"I hope so," he said. "A man like you—you and me—" He winked. "After all, we ain't both wearing berets fer nothing."

"True," I said. "Consider your tip doubled. Now drive away into the sunrise and forget you ever saw me."

He got into the car, beaming, and left. I turned and sized up the Delta Labs.

There was nothing fancy about the place; it consisted of low brick-and-steel buildings, mud, a fence and a guard who was looking at me.

I sauntered over. "I'm from Iowa City," I said. "Now, the rest of the group didn't come—said they'd rather rest one day. But I like to see it all. After all, I paid—"

"Just a minute," the guard said, holding up a palm. "You must be lost, fella. This here ain't no tourist attraction. You can't come in here."

"This *is* the cameo works?" I said anxiously.

He shook his head. "Too bad you let your cab go. It's an hour yet till the bus comes."

A blue-painted staff car came into view, slowed and swung wide to turn in. I fingered the driver's mind. The car swerved, braked to a halt. A portly man in the back leaned forward, frowning. I touched him. He relaxed. The driver leaned across and opened the door. I went around and got in. The guard was watching, open-mouthed.

I gave him a two-finger salute, and the car pulled through the gate.

"Stop in front of the electronics section," I told the corporal at the wheel. The car pulled up. I got out, went up the steps and pushed through the double glass doors. The car sat for a moment, then moved slowly off. The passenger would be wondering why the driver had stopped—but the driver wouldn't remember.

I was inside the building now; that was a start. I didn't like robbery in broad daylight, but it was a lot easier this way. I wasn't equal to climbing any walls or breaking down any locked door—not until I'd had a transfusion, a skin graft and about three months' vacation on a warm beach somewhere.

A man in a white smock emerged from a door. He started past me, spun—

"I'm here about the garbage," I said. "Damn fools *will* put the cans in with the edible. Are you the one called?"

"How's that?" he said after he got his jaw back up.

"I ain't got all the morning!" I shrilled. "You scientist fellers are all alike. Which way is the watchamacallit—equipment lab?"

"Right along there." He pointed. I didn't bother to thank him. It wouldn't have been in character.

A thin man with a brush mustache eyed me sharply as I pushed through the door. I looked at him, nodded absently. "Carry on with your work," I said. "The audit will be carried out in such a way as to disturb you as little as possible. Just show me your voucher file, if you please."

He sighed and waved me toward a filing cabinet. I went to it and pulled a drawer open, glancing about the room. Full shelves were visible through an inner door.

Twenty minutes later I left the building, carrying a sheet-metal carton containing the electronic components I needed to build a matter transmitter—except for the parts like the Möbius coil I'd have to fabricate myself from raw materials. The load was heavy—too heavy for me to carry very far. I parked it at the door and waited until a pickup truck came along.

It pulled over. The driver climbed out and came up the walk to me. "Are you—uh . . . ?" He scratched his head.

"Right." I waved at my loot. "Put it in the back." He obliged. Together we rolled toward the gate. The guard held up his hand, came forward to check the truck. He looked surprised when he saw me.

"Just who are you, fella?" he said.

I didn't like tampering with people any more than I had to. It was a lot like stealing from a blind man: easy, but nothing to feel proud of. I gave him a light touch—just the suggestion that what I would say would be full of deep meaning.

"You know—the regular Wednesday shipment," I said darkly. "Keep it quiet. We're all relying on you."

"Sure thing," he said, stepping back. We gunned through the gate. I glanced back to see him looking after the truck, thinking about the Wednesday shipment on a Friday. He decided it was logical, nodded his head and forgot the whole thing.

13

I'd been riding high for a couple of hours, enjoying the success of the tricks I'd stolen from the Gool.

Now I suddenly felt like something the student morticians had been practicing on. I guided my driver through a second-rate residential section, looking for an M.D. shingle on a front lawn.

The one I found didn't inspire much confidence—you could hardly see it for the weeds—but I didn't want to make a big splash. I had to have an assist from my driver to make it to the front door. He got me inside, parked my box beside me and went off to finish his rounds, under the impression that it had been a dull morning.

The doctor was a seedy, seventyish G.P. with a gross tremor of the hands that a good belt of Scotch would have helped. He looked at me as though I'd interrupted something that was either more fun or paid better than anything I was likely to come up with.

"I need my dressing changed, Doc," I said. "And maybe a shot to keep me going."

"I'm not a dope peddler," he snapped. "You've got the wrong place."

"Just a little medication—whatever's usual. It's a burn."

"Who told you to come here?"

I looked at him meaningfully. "The word gets around."

He glared at me, gnashed his plates, then gestured toward a black-varnished door. "Go right in there."

He gaped at my arm when the bandages were off. I took a quick glance and wished I hadn't.

"How did you do this?"

"Smoking in bed," I said. "Have you got . . . something that . . ."

He caught me before I hit the floor, got me into a

chair. Then he had that Scotch he'd been wanting, gave a shot as an afterthought, and looked at me narrowly.

"I suppose you fell out of that same bed and broke your leg," he said.

"Right. Hell of a dangerous bed."

"I'll be right back." He turned to the door. "Don't go away. I'll just . . . get some gauze."

"Better stay here, Doc. There's plenty of gauze right on that table."

"See here—"

"Skip it, Doc. I know all about you."

"What?"

"I said *all* about you."

He set to work then; a guilty conscience is a tough argument to answer.

He plastered my arm with something and re-wrapped it, then looked over and made a couple of adjustments to the brace. He clucked over the stitches in my scalp, dabbed something on them that hurt like hell, then shoved an old-fashioned stickpin needle into my good arm.

"That's all I can do for you," he said. He handed me a bottle of pills. "Here are some tablets to take in an emergency. Now get out."

"Call me a cab, Doc."

14

I listened while he called, then lit a cigarette and watched through the curtains. After the doc hung up, he came over and stood by me, worrying his upper plate and eyeing me. So far I hadn't had to tinker with his mind, but it would be a good idea to check. I felt my way delicately.

—oh, God, why did I . . . long time ago . . . Mary ever knew . . . go to Arizona, start again, too old . . . I saw the nest of fears that gnawed at him, the frustration and the faint flicker of hope, sick, but not quite dead. I touched his mind, wiped away scars . . .

"Here's your car," he said. He opened the door, looking at me. I started past him.

"Are you sure you're all right?" he said.

"Sure, Pop. And don't worry. Everything's going to be okay."

The driver put my boxes on the back seat. I got in beside him and told him to take me to a men's clothing store. He waited while I changed my hand-me-downs for an off-the-hook suit, new shirt and underwear and a replacement beret. It was the only kind of hat that wouldn't hurt. My issue shoes were still good, but I traded them in on a new pair, added a light raincoat, and threw in a sturdy suitcase for good measure. The clerk said something about money and I dropped an idea into his mind, paused long enough to add a memory of a fabulous night with a redhead. He hardly noticed me leaving.

I tried not to feel like a shoplifter. After all, it's not every day a man gets a chance to swap drygoods for dreams.

In the cab, I transferred my belongings to the new suitcase, then told the driver to pull up at an anonymous-looking hotel. A four-star admiral with frayed cuffs helped me inside with my luggage. The hackie headed for the bay to get rid of the empty box under the impression I was a heavy tipper.

I had a meal in my room, a hot bath, and treated myself to a three-hour nap. I woke up feeling as though those student embalmers might graduate after all.

I thumbed through the phone book and dialed a number.

"I want a Cadillac or Lincoln," I said. "A new one—not the one you rent for funerals—and a driver who won't mind missing a couple of nights' sleep. And put a bed pillow and a blanket in the car."

I went down to the coffee room then for a light meal. I had just finished a cigarette when the car arrived—a dark-blue heavyweight with a high polish and a low silhouette.

"We're going to Denver," I told the driver. "We'll make one stop tomorrow—I have a little shopping to do. I figure about twenty hours. Take a break every hundred miles, and hold it under ninety."

He nodded. I got in the back and sank down in the smell of expensive upholstery.

"I'll cross town and pick up I one-oh-one at—"

"I leave the details to you," I said. He pulled out into the traffic and I got the pillow settled under me and closed my eyes. I'd need all the rest I could get on this trip. I'd heard that compared with the Denver

Records Center, Fort Knox was a cinch. I'd find out for sure when I got there.

The plan I had in mind wasn't the best I could have concocted under more leisurely circumstances. But with every cop in the country under orders to shoot me on sight, I had to move fast. My scheme had the virtue of unlikeliness. Once I was safe in the central vault—supposed to be the only H-bomb-proof structure ever built—I'd put through a phone call to the outside, telling them to watch a certain spot; say the big desk in the President's office. Then I'd assemble my matter transmitter and drop some little item right in front of the assembled big shots. They'd have to admit I had something—and they'd have to start considering the possibility that I wasn't working for the enemy.

It had been a smooth trip, and I'd caught up on my sleep. Now it was five A.M. and we were into the foothills, half an hour out of Denver. I ran over my lines, planning the trickiest part of the job ahead—the initial approach. I'd listened to a couple of news broadcasts. The FBI was still promising an arrest within hours. I learned that I was lying up, or maybe dead, in the vicinity of Key West, and that the situation was under control. That was fine with me. Nobody would expect me to pop up in Denver, still operating under my own power—and wearing a new suit at that.

The Records Center was north of the city, dug into a mountainside. I steered my chauffeur around the downtown section, out a street lined with dark hamburger joints and unlit recharge stations to where a side road branched off. We pulled up. From here on, things might get dangerous—if I was wrong about how easy it was all going to be. I brushed across the driver's mind. He set the brake and got out.

"Don't know how I came to run out of juice, Mr. Brown," he said apologetically. "We just passed a station but it was closed. I guess I'll just have to hike back into town. I sure am sorry; I never did that before."

I told him it was okay, watched as he strode off into the pre-dawn gloom, then got into the front seat and started up. The gate of the reservation surrounding the Records Center was only a mile away now. I drove slowly, feeling ahead for opposition. There didn't seem to be any. Things were quiet as a poker player with a pat hand. My timing was good.

15

I stopped in front of the gate, under a floodlight and the watchful eye of an M.P. with a shiny black tommy gun held at the ready. He didn't seem surprised to see me. I rolled down the window as he came over to the car.

"I have an appointment inside, Corporal," I said. I touched his mind. "The password is 'hotpoint.'"

He nodded, stepped back, and motioned me in. I hesitated. This was almost too easy. I reached out again . . .

. . . *middle of the night . . . password . . . nice car . . . I wish . . .*

I pulled through the gate and headed for the big parking lot, picking a spot in front of a ramp that led down to a tall steel door. There was no one in sight. I got out, dragging my suitcase. It was heavier now, with the wire and magnets I'd added. I crossed the drive, went up to the doors. The silence was eerie.

I swept the area, searching for minds, found nothing. The shielding, I decided, blanked out everything.

There was a personnel door set in the big panel, with a massive, electronic combination lock. I leaned my head against the door and felt for the mechanism, turning the dial right, left, right . . .

The lock opened. I stepped inside, alert.

Silence, darkness. I reached out, sensed walls, slabs of steel, concrete, intricate mechanisms, tunnels deep in the rock . . .

But no personnel. That was surprising—but I wouldn't waste time questioning my good luck. I followed a corridor, opened another door, massive as a vault, passed more halls, more doors. My footsteps made muffled echoes. I passed a final door and came into the heart of the Records Center.

There were lights in the chamber around the grim, featureless periphery of the central vault. I set the valise on the floor, sat on it and lit a cigarette. So far, so good. The Records Center, I saw, had been overrated. Even without my special knowledge, a clever locksmith could have come this far—or almost. But the big vault was another matter; I analyzed its inner workings, saw that the great integrating lock that secured it would yield only to a complex command from the computer set in the wall opposite the vault door. I smoked my cigarette and, with eyes closed, studied the vault a bit further, worked out the code.

I finished the cigarette, stepped on it, went to the console, began pressing keys, tapping out the necessary formulations. Half an hour later I finished. There was a whine from a servo motor; a crimson light flashed. I turned and saw the valve cycle open, showing a bright-lit tunnel within.

16

I dragged my bag inside, threw the lever that closed the entry behind me. A green light went on. I walked along the narrow passage, lined with gray metal shelves stacked with gray tape drums, descended steps, came into a large chamber fitted out with bunks, a tiny galley, toilet facilities, shelves stocked with food. There was a radio, a telephone and a second telephone, bright red. That would be the hotline to Washington. This was the sanctum sanctorum, where the last survivors could wait out the final holocaust—indefinitely.

I opened the door of a steel cabinet. Radiation suits, tools, instruments. Another held bedding. I found a tape player, tapes—even a shelf of books. I found a first-aid kit and gratefully gave myself a hypo-spray jolt of neurite. My pains receded.

I went on to the next room; there were washtubs, a garbage disposal unit, a drier. There was everything here I needed to keep me alive and even comfortable until I could convince someone up above that I shouldn't be shot on sight.

A heavy door barred the way to the room beyond. I turned a wheel, swung the door back, saw more walls lined with filing cabinets, a blank facade of gray steel; and in the center of the room, alone on a squat table—a yellow plastic case that any Sunday supplement reader would have recognized.

It was a Master Tape, the utter top secret programming document that would direct the Terrestrial defense in case of an alien invasion.

It was almost shocking to see it lying there—unprotected except for the flimsy case. The information it contained could put my world in the palm of the enemy's hand.

The room with the tool kit would be the best place to work, I decided. I brought the suitcase containing the electronic gear back from the outer door where I'd left it, opened it and arranged its contents on the table. According to the Gool these simple components were all I needed. The trick was in knowing how to put them together.

There was work ahead of me now. There were the coils to wind, the intricate antenna arrays to lay out; but before I started, I'd take time to call Kayle—or whoever I could get at the other end of the hotline. They'd be a little startled when I turned up at the heart of the defenses they were trying to shield.

I picked up the receiver and a voice spoke:

"Well, Granthan. So you finally made it."

17

"Here are your instructions," Kayle was saying. "Open the vault door. Come out—stripped—and go to the center of the parking lot. Stand there with your hands over your head. A single helicopter manned by a volunteer will approach and drop a gas canister. It won't be lethal, I promise you that. Once you're unconscious, I'll personally see to it that you're transported to the Institute in safety. Every effort will be made to overcome the Gool conditioning. If we're successful, you'll be awakened. If not..."

He let the sentence hang. It didn't need to be finished. I understood what he meant.

I was listening. I was still not worried. Here, I would be safe against anything until the food ran out—and that wouldn't be for months.

"You're bluffing, Kayle," I said. "You're trying to put the best face on something that you can't control. If you'd—"

"You were careless at Delta Labs, Granthan. There were too many people with odd blanks in their memories and too many unusual occurrences, all on the same day. You tipped your hand. Once we knew what we were up against, it was simply a matter of following you at an adequate distance. We have certain shielding materials, as you know. We tried them all. There's a new one that's quite effective.

"But as I was saying, we've kept you under constant surveillance. When we saw which way you were heading, we just stayed out of sight and let you trap yourself."

"You're lying. Why would you want me here?"

"That's very simple," Kayle said harshly. "It's the finest trap ever built by man—and you're safely in it."

"Safely is right," I told him. "I have everything I need here. And that brings me to my reason for being here—in case you're curious. I'm going to build a matter transmitter. And to prove my good faith, I'll transmit the Master Tape to you. I'll show you that I could have stolen the damned thing if I'd wanted to."

"Indeed? Tell me, Granthan, do you really think we'd be fools enough to leave the Master Tape behind when we evacuated the area?"

"I don't know about that—but it's here."

"Sorry," Kayle said. "You're deluding yourself." His voice was suddenly softer, some of the triumph gone from it. "Don't bother struggling, Granthan. The finest brains in the country have combined to place you where you are. You haven't a chance, except to do as I say. Make it easy on yourself. I have no wish to extend your ordeal."

"You can't touch me, Kayle. This vault is proof against a hell-bomb, and it's stocked for a siege..."

"That's right," Kayle said. His voice sounded tired. "It's proof against a hell-bomb. But what if the hell-bomb's in the vault with you?"

I felt like a demolition man, working to defuse a blockbuster, who's suddenly heard a loud *click!* from the detonator. I dropped the phone, stared around the room. I saw nothing that could be a bomb. I ran to the next room, the one beyond. Nothing. I went back to the phone, grabbed it up.

"You ought to know better than to bluff now, Kayle!" I yelled. "I wouldn't leave this spot now for half a dozen hypothetical hell-bombs!"

"In the center room," Kayle said. "Lift the cover over the floor drain. You'll find it there. You know what they look like. Don't tamper with its mechanism; it's internally trapped. You'll have to take my word for it we didn't bother installing a dummy."

I dropped the phone, hurried to the spot Kayle had described. The bomb casing was there—a dull gray ovoid, with a lifting eye set in the top. It didn't look dangerous. It just lay quietly, waiting...

Back at the telephone, I had trouble finding my voice. "How long?" I croaked.

"It was triggered when you entered the vault," Kayle said. "There's a time mechanism. It's irreversible; you can't force anyone to cancel it. And it's no use your hiding in the outer passages.

"The whole center will be destroyed in the blast. Even *it* can't stand against a bomb buried in its heart. But we'll gladly sacrifice the center to eliminate you."

"How long?"

"I suggest you come out quickly, so that a crew can enter the vault to disarm the bomb."

"How long!"

"When you're ready to emerge, call me." The line went dead.

I put the phone back in its cradle carefully, like a rare and valuable egg.

I tried to think. I'd been charging full-speed ahead ever since I had decided on my scheme of action while

I was still riding the surf off the Florida coast, and I'd stuck to it. Now it had hatched in my face—and the thing that had crawled out wasn't the downy little chick of success. It had teeth and claws and was eyeing me like a basilisk...

But I still had unplayed aces—if there was time.

I had meant to use the matter transmitter to stage a dramatic proof that I wasn't the tool of the enemy. The demonstration would be more dramatic than I had planned. The bomb would fit the machine as easily as the tape. The wheels would be surprised when their firecracker went off—right on schedule—in the middle of the Mojave Desert.

I set to work, my heart pounding. If I could bring this off—if I had time—if the transmitter worked as advertised...

The stolen knowledge flowed smoothly, effortlessly. It was as though I had been assembling matter transmitters for years, knew every step by heart. First the Möbius windings, yard after yard of heavy copper wrapped with precision around a core of carbon; then the power supply, the first and second stage amplimitters...

How long? In the sump in the next room, the bomb lay quietly ticking. How long...?

18

The main assembly was ready now. I laid out cables, tapping my apparatus in to the nuclear power-source

buried under the vault. The demand, for one short
instant, would tax even those mighty engines. I fixed
hooks at the proper points in the room, wove soft
aluminum wire in the correct pattern, curiously like
that of the psychotronic amplifier Reed and I had
designed. I was almost finished now. How long? I
made the last connections, cleared away the litter. The
matter transmitter stood on the table, complete. At
any instant, the bomb would reduce it—and the secret
of its construction—to incandescent gas—unless I
transmitted the bomb out of range first. I turned toward the laundry room—and the telephone rang.

I hesitated, then crossed the room and snatched it
up.

"Listen to me," Kayle said grimly. "Give me
straight, fast answers. You said the Master Tape was
there, in the vault with you. Now tell me: What does
it look like?"

"What?"

"The . . . ah . . . dummy tape. What is its appear-
ance?"

"It's a roughly square plastic container, bright yellow, eighteen inches on a side, about six inches thick.
What about it?"

Kayle's voice sounded strained. "I've made in-
quiries. No one here seems to know the exact present
location of the Master Tape. Each department says
that they were under the impression that another handled the matter. I'm unable to learn who, precisely,
removed the tape from the vault. Now you say there
is a yellow plastic container—"

"I know what the Master Tape looks like," I said.
"This is either it or a hell of a good copy."

"Granthan," Kayle said. There was a note of desperation in his voice now. "There have been some blunders made. I knew you were under the influence of the Gool. It didn't occur to me that I might be too. Why did I make it possible for you to penetrate to the central vault? There were a hundred simpler ways in which I could have dealt with the problem. We're in trouble, Granthan, serious trouble. The tape you have there is genuine. We've all played into the enemy's hands."

"You're wasting valuable time, Kayle," I snapped. "When does the bomb go up?"

"Granthan, there's little time left. Bring the Master Tape and leave the vault—"

"No dice, Kayle, I'm staying until I finish; then—"

"Granthan! If there's anything to your mad idea of such a machine, destroy it! Quickly! Don't you see the Gool would only have given you the secret in order to enable you to steal the tape!"

I cut him off. In the sudden silence, I heard a distant sound—or had I sensed a thought? I strained outward . . .

. . . *volunteered . . . damn fool . . . thing on my head is heavy . . . better work . . .*

. . . *now . . . okay . . . valve, gas . . . kills in a split second they said—then get out . . .*

I stabbed out, pushed through the obscuring veil of masonry, sensed a man in the computer room, dressed in gray coveralls, a grotesque shield over his head and shoulders. He reached for a red-painted valve—

I struck at his mind with just enough force, felt him stagger back, fall. I fumbled in his brain, stim-

ulated the sleep center. He sank deep into unconsciousness. I leaned against the table, weak with the
reaction. Kayle had almost tricked me that time.

I reached out again, swept the area with desperate
urgency. Far away, I sensed the hazy clutter of many
minds, out of range. There was nothing more. The
poisonous gas had been the only threat—except
for the bomb itself. But I had to move fast, before
my time ran out, to transmit the bomb to a desert
area . . .

I paused, stood frozen in mid-move. A desert. What
desert?

The transmitter operated in accordance with as rigid
a set of laws as did the planets swinging in their orbits;
strange laws, but laws of nature nonetheless. No receiver was required. The destination of the mass under
transmission was determined by the operator, holding
in his mind the five-dimensional conceptualization of
the target, guiding the action of the machine.

And I had no target.

I could no more direct the bomb to a desert without
a five-fold grasp of its multiordinal spatial, temporal,
and entropic coordinates than I could fire a rifle at a
target in the dark.

I was like a man with a grenade in his hand, pin
pulled—and locked in a cell.

I swept the exocosm again, desperately. And caught
a thin, live line. I traced it; it cut through the mountain,
dived deep underground, crossed the boundless plain . . .

Never branching, it bored on, turning upward
now—and ending.

I rested, gathering strength, then probed, straining . . .

There was a room, men. I recognized Kayle, gray-faced, haggard. A tall man in braided blue stood near him. Others stood silently by, tension on every face. Maps covered the wall behind them.

I was looking into the War Room at the Pentagon in Washington. The line I had traced was the telephonic hotline, the top-security link between the Records Center and the command level. It was a heavy cable, well protected and always open. It would free me from the trap. With Gool-tutored skill I scanned the room, memorized its coordinates. Then I withdrew.

Like a swimmer coming up from a long dive, I fought my way back to the level of immediate awareness. I sagged into a chair, blinking at the drab walls, the complexity of the transmitter. I must move fast now, place the bomb in the transmitter's field, direct it at the target. With an effort I got to my feet, went to the sump, lifted the cover. I grasped the lifting eye—the thing was heavy—and the bomb came up, out onto the floor. I dragged it to the transmitter...

And only then realized what I'd been about to do. My target.

The War Room—the nerve center of Earth's defenses. And I had been ready to dump the hell-bomb there. In my frenzy to be rid of it I would have played into the hands of the Gool.

19

I went to the phone.

"Kayle! I guess you've got a recorder on the line.

I'll give you the details of the transmitter circuits. It's complicated, but fifteen minutes ought to—"

"No time," Kayle cut in. "I'm sorry about everything, Granthan. If you've finished the machine, it's a tragedy for humanity—if it works. I can only ask you to try—when the Gool command comes—not to give them what they want. I'll tell you, now, Granthan. The bomb blows in"—there was a pause—"two minutes and twenty-one seconds. Try to hold them off. If you can stand against them for that long at least—"

I slammed the phone down, cold sweat popping out across my face. Two minutes . . . too late for anything. The men in the War Room would never know how close I had come to beating the Gool—and them.

But I could still save the Master Tape. I wrestled the yellow plastic case that housed the tape onto the table, into the machine.

And the world vanished in a blaze of darkness, a clamor of silence.

NOW, MASTERS! NOW! LINK UP! LINK UP!

Like a bad dream coming back in daylight, I felt the obscene presence of massed Gool minds, attenuated by distance but terrible in their power, probing, thrusting, clutching at me. I fought back, struggling against paralysis, trying to gather my strength, use what I had learned . . .

SEE, MASTERS, HOW IT WOULD ELUDE US. BLANK IT OFF, TOGETHER NOW . . .

The paths closed before me. My mind writhed, twisted, darted here and there—and met only the impenetrable shield of the Gool defenses.

IT TIRES, MASTERS. WORK SWIFTLY NOW. LET US

IMPRESS ON THE SUBJECT THE COORDINATES OF THE
BRAIN PIT. The conceptualization drifted into my
mind. HERE, MAN. TRANSMIT THE TAPE HERE!

As from a distance, my monitor Personality Fraction watched the struggle. Kayle had been right. The
Gool had waited—and now their movement had come.
Even my last impulse of defiance—to place the tape
in the machine—to transmit it to the War Room—
had been at the Gool command. They had looked into
my mind. They understood psychology as no human
analyst ever could; and they had led me in the most
effective way possible, by letting me believe I was
the master. They had made use of my human ingenuity
to carry out their wishes—and Kayle had made it easy
for them by evacuating a twenty-mile radius around
me, leaving the field clear for the Gool.

HERE—the Gool voice rang like a bell in my mind—
TRANSMIT THE TAPE HERE!

Even as I fought against the impulse to comply, I
felt my arm twitch toward the machine.

THROW THE SWITCH! the voice thundered.

I struggled, willed my arm to stay at my side. Only
a minute longer, I thought. Only a minute more, and
the bomb would save me . . .

LINK UP, MASTERS!

I WILL NOT LINK. YOU PLOT TO FEED AT MY EX-
PENSE.

NO! BY THE MOTHER WORM, I PLEDGE MY GROOVE
AT THE EATING TROUGH. FOR US THE STRANGELIFE WILL
GUT THE GREAT VAULT OF ITS NEST WORLD!

ALREADY YOU BLOAT AT OUR EXPENSE!

FOOLS! WOULD YOU BICKER NOW? LINK UP!

20

The Gool raged—and I grasped for an elusive thought and held it.

With infinite sluggishness, I moved.

LINK UP, MASTERS: THEN ALL WILL FEED . . .

IT IS A TRICK. I WILL NOT LINK.

I found the bomb, fumbled for a grip.

DISASTER IMPENDS, MY MASTERS! NOW IS THE PRIZE LOST TO US, UNLESS YOU JOIN WITH ME!

My breath choked off in my throat; a hideous pain coiled outward from my chest. But it was unimportant. Only the bomb mattered. I tottered, groping. There was the table; the transmitter . . .

I lifted the bomb, felt the half-healed skin of my burned arm crackle as I strained . . .

I thrust the case containing the Master Tape out of the field of the transmitter, then pushed, half rolled the bomb into position. I groped for the switch, found it. I tried to draw breath, felt only a surge of agony. Blackness was closing in . . .

The coordinates . . .

From the whirling fog of pain and darkness, I brought the target concept of the Gool cavern into view, clarified it, held it . . .

MASTERS! HOLD THE MAN! DISASTER!

Then I felt the Gool, their suspicions yielding to the panic in the mind of the Prime Overlord, link their power against me. I stood paralyzed, felt my identity dissolving like water pouring from a smashed pot. I tried to remember—but it was too faint, too far away.

Then from somewhere a voice seemed to cut in, the calm voice of an emergency reserve Personality Fraction. "You are under attack. Activate the reserve plan. Level Five. Use Level Five. Act now. Use Level Five . . ."

Through the miasma of Gool pressure, I felt the hairs stiffen on the back of my neck. All around me the Gool voices raged, a swelling symphony of discord. But they were nothing. Level Five . . .

There was no turning back. The compulsions were there, acting even as I drew in a breath to howl my terror—

Level Five. Down past the shapes of dreams, the intense faces of hallucination; Level Three; Level Four and the silent ranked memories . . . and deeper still—

Into a region of looming, gibbering horror, of shadowy moving shapes of evil, of dreaded presences that lurked at the edge of vision . . .

Down amid the clamor of voiceless fears, the mounting hungers, the reaching claws of all that man had feared since the first tailless primate screamed out his terror in a treetop: the fear of falling, the fear of heights.

Down to Level Five. Nightmare level.

21

I groped outward, found the plane of Contact—and hurled the weight of man's ancient fears at the waiting Gool—and in their black confining caves deep in the rock of a far world, they felt the roaring tide of fear— fear of the dark, and of living burial. The horrors in man's secret mind confronted the horrors of the Gool Brain Pit. And I felt the Gool break, retreat in blind panic from me—

All but one. The Prime Overlord reeled back with the rest, but his was a mind of terrible power. I sensed for a moment his bloated immense form, the seething gnawing hungers, insatiable, never to be appeased. Then he rallied—but he was alone now.

LINK UP, MASTERS! THE PRIZE IS LOST, KILL THE STRANGELIFE! KILL THE STRANGELIFE!

I felt a knife at my heart. It fluttered—and stopped. And in that instant, I broke past his control, threw the switch. There was the sharp crack of imploding air. Then I was floating down, ever down, and all sensation was far away.

MASTERS! KILL TH—

The pain cut off in an instant of profound silence and utter dark.

Then sound roared in my ears, and I felt the harsh impact of the floor against my face as I fell, and then I knew nothing more.

22

"I hope," General Titus was saying, "that you'll accept the decoration now, Mr. Granthan. It will be the first time in history that a civilian has been accorded this honor—and you deserve it."

I was lying in a clean white bed, propped up by big soft pillows, with a couple of good-looking nurses hovering a few feet away. I was in a mood to tolerate even Titus.

"Thanks, General," I said. "I suggest you give the medal to the volunteer who came in to gas me. He knew what he was going up against; I didn't."

"It's over now, Granthan," Kayle said. He attempted to beam, settled for a frosty smile. "You surely understand—"

"Understanding," I said. "That's all we need to turn this planet—and a lot of other ones—into the kind of worlds the human mind needs to expand into."

"You're tired, Granthan," Kayle said. "You get some rest. In a few weeks you'll be back on the job, as good as new."

"That's where the key is," I said. "In our minds; there's so much there, and we haven't even scratched the surface. To the mind nothing is impossible. Matter is an illusion, space and time are just convenient fictions—"

"I'll leave the medal here, Mr. Granthan. When you feel equal to it, we'll make the official presentation. Television . . ."

He faded off as I closed my eyes and thought about things that had been clamoring for attention ever since I'd met the Gool, but hadn't had time to explore. My arm...

I felt my way along it—from inside—tracing the area of damage, watching as the bodily defenses worked away, toiling to renew, replace. It was a slow, mindless process. But if I helped a little...

It was easy. The pattern was there. I felt the tissues renew themselves, the skin regenerate.

The bone was more difficult. I searched out the necessary minerals, diverted blood; the broken ends knit....

The nurse was bending over me, a bowl of soup in her hand.

23

"You've been asleep for a long time, sir," she said, smiling. "How about some nice chicken broth now?"

I ate the soup and asked for more. A doctor came and peeled back my bandages, did a double-take, and rushed away. I looked. The skin was new and pink, like a baby's—but it was all there. I flexed my right leg; there was no twinge of pain.

I listened for a while as the doctors gabbled, clucked, probed and made pronouncements. Then I closed my eyes again. I thought about the matter transmitter. The government was sitting on it, of course. A military secret of the greatest importance, Titus called it. Maybe

someday the public would hear about it; in the mean-
time—

"How about letting me out of here?" I said suddenly. A pop-eyed doctor with a fringe of gray hair
blinked at me, went back to fingering my arm. Kayle
hove into view.

"I want out," I said. "I'm recovered, right? So now
just give me my clothes."

"Now, now, just relax, Granthan. You know it's
not as simple as that. There are a lot of matters we
must go over."

"The war's over," I said. "You admitted that. I
want out."

"Sorry." Kayle shook his head. "That's out of the
question."

"Doc," I said. "Am I well?"

"Yes," he said. "Amazing case. You're as fit as
you'll ever be; I've never—"

"I'm afraid you'll have to resign yourself to being
here for a while longer, Granthan," Kayle said. "After
all, we can't—"

"Can't let the secret of matter transmission run
around loose eh? So until you figure out the angles,
I'm a prisoner, right?"

"I'd hardly call it that, Granthan. Still . . ."

I closed my eyes. The matter transmitter—a strange
device. A field, not distorting space, but accentuating
certain characteristics of a matter field in space-time,
subtly shifting relationships . . .

Just as the mind could compare unrelated data,
draw from them new concepts, new parallels . . .

The circuits of the matter transmitter . . . and the
patterns of the mind . . .

The exocosm and the endocosm, like the skin and the orange, everywhere in contact...

Somewhere there was a beach of white sand, and dunes with graceful sea oats that leaned in a gentle wind. There was blue water to the far horizon, and a blue sky, and nowhere were there any generals with medals and television cameras, or flint-eyed bureaucrats with long schemes...

And with this gentle folding... thus...

And a pressure here... so...

I opened my eyes, raised myself on one elbow— and saw the sea. The sun was hot on my body, but not too hot, and the sand was white as sugar. Far away, a seagull tilted, circling.

A wave rolled in, washed my foot in cool water.

I lay on my back, and looked up at white clouds in a blue sky, and smiled—then laughed aloud.

Distantly the seagull's cry echoed my laughter.

24

As Margrave finished the last page of the transcript, he snorted, jabbed savagely at the talk box and muttered to himself.

"Insolence! Damned civilian made jackasses out of Kayle and his whole damn security apparatus." He swiveled hard as his aide hurried in.

"Freddy!" he barked. "I want this wise guy picked up *right now*. This afternoon—or whatever it is out there in Borneo or wherever. Have him brought here under close arrest—I don't want any slipups! After that fiasco in Denver, I don't know what to expect. This fellow seems to have learned some tricks, if half of what he told Security is true." He prodded the transcript. "I want this classified Ultimate Top Secret, and put in my personal safe. I specifically don't want Kayle to see it. Kill any other copies."

"This is the sole copy, Admiral," Freddy reassured the agitated officer. "I haven't read it myself, of course. I shall caution Cincpac to take appropriate action regarding the original recordings, and the personnel involved."

"Do that! Fast!" the admiral commanded. "I don't like anything about this affair, Freddy," he added. "I want this Granthan squashed like a bug!"

25

Granthan was reclining at ease in the relatively cool evening breeze on the shady veranda of the Old Colonial Hotel. He was sipping a tall drink called the Tropical Sunset, and admiring the real thing now dyeing the sky purple and gold, silhouetting tall coconut palms. There was a sound from the left; Granthan glanced that way and saw skinny legs in khaki shorts, broad island faces under solar topis, the glint of badges and holstered pistols. Hobnailed boots were *clump-clump!*ing toward him from both directions. The man in the lead, a wiry Caucasian with a power pistol in his hand, caught Granthan's eye and said:

"Don't move a muscle, mister, or I'll blow off your kneecap. They want you alive," he explained, almost apologetically.

Granthan closed his eyes, reviewed certain patterns in his mind, aligned them, then let his thoughts roam over remembered scenes: an icy slope near the peak of Mount Kabulu; late sunlight slanting in dusty bars through the high foliage of immense redwoods; a tranquil vista of ripples on a pond, seen through a screen of young tree trunks; a gallery wall with a well-lit painting showing a village street in France a century ago, and signed "Pissaro"; he was seated at a table on a quiet terrace with a view over a garden with a complex pattern of flower beds and paths lined with dark-green borders of ground juniper. A Puccini aria emanated gently from an invisible source.

"Beg pardon, sir, I didn't see you come in," a diffident voice spoke at his elbow. A waiter in formal livery offered a folio-sized menu.

Granthan called for a phone, dialed Colonel Kayle's classified number; when the security man came on the line, Granthan said without preamble:

"Your boys drew a blank at the hotel. Don't blame them; they sneaked up on me in good style, but let's face it; I'm not going to be anybody's prisoner, so call 'em off and save the taxpayers' dollars. I don't owe you anything at all, Kayle, and I choose to live as I please, without even any medals. Better write me off. Don't bother tracing the call; I won't be here. Ta."

26

A quarter of an hour later, Admiral-General Margrave was fixing Commander Phipps with a steely glare. "I want this whole incident killed, Freddy," he said in Doomsday tones. "All of it, from the last contact with *Belshazzar*. See to it that Granthan is placed under Class One quarantine. Then get hold of Kayle and get him here pronto. Do it!"

27

It was almost dawn when a haggard Colonel Kayle was ushered into the Presence. Margrave barked at him to sit.

"Admiral, sir," Kayle blurted. "I can't be held responsible for Granthan and his crazy activities. I was against—"

"Don't tell me who I can hold responsible for what, Art," Margrave cut him off. "It's plain to see that our whole conception of security has to be overhauled. There's no way one can control a man who can disappear and pop up elsewhere anytime he pleases."

"Right, sir," Granthan's voice spoke in the momentary silence. He stepped into view from the admiral's lavatory. "So the first thing to do under the circumstances is to tell me what you want from me, and if possible, I'll oblige."

Margrave half rose from his chair, looking almost appealingly at Kayle. The latter's hand went toward his holstered sidearm, then pulled out cigarettes instead.

"What I want from you, Mr. Granthan," the admiral said heavily, "is for all of this not to have happened."

"Time travel?" Granthan queried. He took one of Kayle's cigarettes, lit it and nodded.

"All right, sir," he said briskly to Margrave. "I'll see what I can do. Meanwhile forget all about me. Deal?" He extended his hand.

"By God, it's a deal, Mr. Granthan," the admiral said fervently. "Absolutely confidential, of course," he added. "Kayle," he went on, favoring the Security man with a pitying look, "drop Mr. Granthan from your files. Completely; permanently." He sighed. "Granthan, if any word of this gets out, I'll see to it you never have another peaceful hour in your life. On the other hand . . ." He let it trail off.

"Don't worry, Admiral," Granthan reassured the senior officer, "I doubt very much that I'll succeed."

"Amen," Margrave said fervently. "Meanwhile, call on Colonel Kayle for whatever you need. Art," he transferred his attention to the colonel, "anything Mr. Granthan asks for—absolutely anything. Report to me daily." He looked again, warily, at Granthan.

"Good-bye, sir," he said. "I can only pray you're a patriot."

"No fear, Admiral," Granthan replied steadily. "I'd even prefer Art here breathing down my neck to another brush with the Gool—even in the past. So long, gentlemen. At least I'm sure it will be interesting." He turned and left the room. Margrave and Kayle looked at each other. Both seemed about to speak, but neither did. At last Kayle found his voice:

"It never happened. None of it."

"What never happened?" Margrave inquired in a tone of mild interest.

"Beats me, sir," Kayle said in a defeated tone.

"On the strength of that report, General," Margrave said, "I feel quite justified in assuring you your star will be on your shoulder no later than tomorrow. As for myself, I've been holding my retirement papers for some time now. I think I'm ready to send them through. Just be sure to give special priority treatment to any requests that come through from one Peter Granthan, Ph.D."

ACE
SCIENCE FICTION
SPECIALS

Under the brilliant editorship of Terry Carr,
the award-winning <u>Ace Science Fiction Specials</u>
were <u>the</u> imprint for literate, quality sf.

Now, once again under the leadership of Terry Carr,
<u>The New Ace SF Specials</u> have been created
to seek out the talents and titles that will lead
science fiction into the 21st Century.

__ THE WILD SHORE	88871-2/$2.95	
Kim Stanley Robinson		
__ GREEN EYES	30274-2/$2.95	
Lucius Shepard		
__ NEUROMANCER	56957-9/$2.95	
William Gibson		
__ PALIMPSESTS	65065-1/$2.95	
Carter Scholz and Glenn Harcourt		
__ THEM BONES	80557-4/$2.95	
Howard Waldrop		
__ IN THE DRIFT	35869-1/$2.95	
Michael Swanwick		

Prices may be slightly higher in Canada

BESTSELLING
Science Fiction
and
Fantasy

☐ 47810-7	**THE LEFT HAND OF DARKNESS,** Ursula K. Le Guin	$2.95
☐ 16021-2	**DORSAI!,** Gordon R. Dickson	$2.95
☐ 80583-3	**THIEVES' WORLD,**™ Robert Lynn Asprin, editor	$2.95
☐ 11456-3	**CONAN #1,** Robert E. Howard, L. Sprague de Camp, Lin Carter	$2.75
☐ 49142-1	**LORD DARCY INVESTIGATES,** Randall Garrett	$2.75
☐ 21889-X	**EXPANDED UNIVERSE,** Robert A. Heinlein	$3.95
☐ 87330-8	**THE WARLOCK UNLOCKED,** Christopher Stasheff	$2.95
☐ 05490-0	**BERSERKER,** Fred Saberhagen	$2.95
☐ 10264-6	**CHANGELING,** Roger Zelazny	$2.95
☐ 51553-3	**THE MAGIC GOES AWAY,** Larry Niven	$2.95

Prices may be slightly higher in Canada.
